Season of Change

A novel

Maryann Sawka

It's Your Day
Publishing

A Maryann Sawka novel for It's Your Day Publishing

Season of Change. Copyright © 2023 by

It's Your Day Publishing, LLC

It's Your Day
Publishing

Instagram: @ItsYourDayPublishing

Instagram: @maryannbsawka

Email: Itsyourdaypublishing@gmail.com

Cover design by It's Your Day Publishing

Cover photograph Coverjig.com

ISBN: 9798852905086

For Eli, Megan and Sarah

For my mom

CHAPTER 1

Opening the front door, Jillian tossed her suitcase, laptop bag and trusty Michael Kors satchel down in the foyer and breathed a sigh of relief as she crossed into the living room. Snuggling into the stark white sofa, she kicked off her shoes to stretch her toes that were cramped from wearing the heels she had put on very early that morning. It had been a long day and an even longer week of travel. Though she loved her job and was good at it, the heavy travel schedule could be exhausting and didn't leave much time for anything but work.

She'd been on the road most weeks for the past several months, flying home Friday night and back out Sunday evening to another client visit or conference. Jillian usually saw her world passing by as the sun dipped out of sight from 35,000 feet. She watched families and singles and grandparents waiting for loved ones to arrive or wishing them goodbye. Sometimes she felt a pang of jealousy at the family life she put on hold while she built her career. It was her choice and a good one at this time in her life, but that didn't mean it didn't hurt a little sometimes, too. But, she was home and glad for it.

Every so often, when she was away and alone, she thought

of her younger sister and her lively family of four, with her husband and son and daughter. Jillian relished being an aunt, but sometimes longed to be a mother. However, the corporate ladder was long and she was just hitting the middle rung of success. She knew the schedule and time commitments when she accepted the position of senior account manager for a young, thriving consulting company. Here, she was building her brand as the company built theirs. Her brand was what she wanted people to think of when they heard her name. Jillian Simmons - efficient, strategic and focused leader.

For the most part, it was a good job with options for advancement. She worked hard and had proven herself over the past couple of years and she was just getting started.

Even with all of the travel and strong work ethic, she managed to find time for her boyfriend, Kevin, the VP of Account Acquisitions at her company. Smart, handsome, wealthy and mostly fun, he was also her boss. She worried about that obvious conflict, but he convinced her it wouldn't pose a problem for them since they both traveled extensively. And that's why he's so good at his job, she thought with a rueful smile. He was well respected and known for sealing the deal. Wonder if he looked at their relationship as just another deal to seal, she thoughtfully considered, looking around the townhouse they shared.

They say opposites attract, she thought, looking at the elegant décor and furnishings, and that never more evident than in their relationship. Jillian was a simple and grounded woman, not out to impress anyone, but with integrity in everything she does. If she's assigned a task, she works it as though she'll unveil her results to the president. In doing so, she sometimes sacrifices parts of herself.

On the other hand, Kevin was a flashy person who was mostly into himself and his appearance, thinking he has a certain image to maintain. She can't argue, though, since in many ways he's just as important as the CEO of their company, who happens to be his cousin. With his classic movie star good looks, tanned skin, blonde hair and blazing blue eyes, it's no wonder Kevin is one of the most eligible bachelors in the office. His past exploits are a favorite topic of the rumor mill, another reason she took a beat to think before going out with him. But, as she reminded herself, that was before they started dating. Everyone knows they're involved, so would-be suitors are kept at bay. She sometimes thinks the travel helps keep their relationship balanced since they aren't often in the same city at the same time. Distance makes the heart grow fonder, she thinks, with a smile.

Jillian has lived on her own since graduating college. Now, at 29, she's sharing a household with Kevin, who insisted that she move in with him and save the rent money she was throwing away since her time as a road warrior meant her apartment was vacant more often than it was occupied. She sometimes found it challenging to find time for herself when at home. Downtime wasn't plentiful, between a demanding job and a somewhat demanding boyfriend. Their relationship wasn't as strong these days as it had been in the beginning, but she wasn't ready to throw in the towel just yet.

"Hello," she called out as she walked around the townhouse. It was a lovely two-story unit with an expansive patio in the rear and modern décor that wouldn't have been her first choice. Since it was Kevin's house, she wasn't involved in choosing the décor, but could think of a few changes she'd make if given the opportunity, eyeing the colorful art deco painting in the foyer. Her style was more cozy comfort, cottage like with soft hues and a few pops of color. If you didn't know that someone occupied the townhouse, some might mistake it as a show unit for prospective buyers.

"Hi," Kevin called from his office on the second floor as she reached the top of the stairs taking in the familiar, yet breathtaking view of the back yard through the large window.

She reached the office and paused to study him from the doorway. He was bent over his MacBook, his expression intent with his eyebrows knit in a look she recognized as his concentration expression. His hair had a slightly tousled look, an indication he'd run his hands through it several times. There was a slight hunch to his shoulder as he sternly surveyed a spreadsheet.

She noticed he was working on his expense report from his last business trip, a daunting task of receipts and calendar entries. They did their expense reports electronically, then signed them with a mouse click and sent them to payroll for processing. Usually she did both of theirs, but he had to fend for himself this week while she was out of town and he wasn't. It took him longer to weed through the charge codes and project numbers while she was a whiz at figuring it all out. She often thought if he had a secretary, the only thing he'd do to complete his expense reports would be to click on his signature. That may have even been too much for him, she laughed to herself.

She reached around the desk, placed her arms around his neck from behind and planted a kiss on the top of his head.

"Babe, I'm a little busy now," he said, reaching up to pull her into his lap with a playful smile, kissing her neck with a groan. "Jilly, I have to get this done today since I…"

"Since you procrastinated all week, right?" she laughed, knowing him well and glad he was in such a playful mood.

"Exactly!" he said pushing her upright with a little slap on her rear as she laughed on her way out of his office.

"How was your trip?" he called to her retreating figure.

"All good…I won the account, so we're expanding our footprint while helping Morton Enterprises do the same. I still have to finalize the details, but all looks good. They were impressed with our reorganization strategy especially since it doesn't include any reduction in their workforce. I presented more of an allocation of their current resources and they liked it."

"Who did you meet with this time? Was the whole board there or did you meet with Ryan and his team?" he asked.

"I met with Ryan first, reviewed the plans and addressed the concerns he had, then I presented it to the board. You remember the handholding that comes with managing accounts. So much of what I do is relationship management, I don't mind the little extras if it helps seal the deal."

"As long as those little extras don't include anything else," he teased, barely hiding his jealous streak that showed up every so often, even if her work was all for the sake of their company.

"Don't worry, Ryan was a perfect gentleman."

After unpacking and taking a long, luxurious bath, she changed into a sundress, poured a glass of ice cold sparkling peach Moscato and settled on the back deck to wait for Kevin. The evening was warm and she could see the lightening bugs starting to pop here and there, the perfect compliment to the choir of summer insects chirping in the twilight. Breathing in a deep sigh, she smiled and turned to answer her cell.

"Ann, what's going on?" she answered, still smiling, as she pictured her best friend probably still at her office. Ann was more of a workaholic than Jillian, if that was even possible.

"Oh, just wrapping a few things at work. Wanted to see if you wanted to grab a coffee tomorrow morning to catch-up. I haven't laid eyes on you in weeks, girl!" Ann responded in her usual sassy way.

"Yeah, that sounds great Ann. I'll meet you at 10?." Jillian said, excited to see her friend.

Kevin strolled out to join her as she finished her call, "What do you want to do for dinner? Go out or order in?"

Snuggling in next to him on the outdoor sofa, "Hmm…I could go for a pizza with pepperoni and mushroom. I don't feel like going back out after I just got home. What do you think?"

He kissed her temple, smoothing her hair back as he dialed-up their favorite pizzeria.

The next morning, Jillian slept-in a bit longer than usual,

relishing the feeling of not having to set an alarm this weekend. She had plenty of time for a quick run and shower before she met Ann. Kevin was already gone she noticed, wondering what got him up and out of the house so early. After devouring their pizza and watching a movie, they got reacquainted well into the night, dozing off in each other arms after until they both turned onto their sides to catch a few hours of sleep. As much as he liked to hold her while he slept, she could never get comfortable like that, feeling trapped. She usually waited until she heard his soft breathing turn to snores before shifting out of his embrace.

Strolling into the coffee shop, she looked around for Ann, but didn't see her as she settled into a small table to wait for her friend. Looking around, she marveled at how people from all walks of life frequented the shop, either lingering over coffee with a book or hustling their kids to place their orders before they rushed back out to a Saturday morning soccer game. The sports families reminded her of her sister, imagining them doing the same thing right about now. There were a few college kids discussing their recent midterms, some still hurting from a hangover by the looks of them. That's what she loves about this place. It's a place where everyone is welcome and happily milling about their days in their own worlds. Old, young and hungover looking for a cup of coffee to get their day started. With the sun shining brightly, she inhaled the fresh coffee scent mingled with a chocolate scent from the baked goods in the glass cabinet as the ceiling fans lazily moved the sweet scents through the air.

"Girl! Where have you been?" Ann cried, rushing through the door to grab her in a big hug before Jillian could even get out of her seat.

With a laugh, she returned the tight hug, once again grateful for her friendship over the years. "So good to see you, Ann!"

"Did you order?"

"No, I was waiting for your late self to deign me with your presence, you know, us peasants," Jillian laughed, her tone automatically switching to humor as she took in her friend's appearance. Never one to be seen "undone," Ann was sporting a full face of flawless makeup, Lululemon leggings with a matching yoga jacket and squeaky clean Hoka running shoes that had probably never seen a running path.

Settling with their coffees and pastries, the old friends spent an hour or so catching up. "So, when do you think Kevin is going to get off his ass and put a ring on it?" Ann demanded as Jillian let out a bark of a laugh. Not many people could get away with talking about or to Kevin like that. The two of them have had more than one shouting match since Jillian moved in with him. Ann always remarked that she couldn't help it that it was the Sicilian coming out of her when she challenged him. Taking it all in good fun, he usually laughed off Ann's protectiveness of Jillian, but she could always sense when it was getting too heated and dialed it down for Jillian's sake.

CHAPTER 2

The days flew by in a whirl, days turning into weeks and weeks turning into more client visits. She was still working with Ryan on the final implementation of their reallocation strategy they had finally settled on. Ryan was a great partner, but she spent as much time reassuring him about the changes they were implementing as she did flying back and forth to his office.

With a slight smile, she remembered her last dinner with Ryan, when he suggested a nightcap in her room after they finished a late supper and a couple bottles of wine. She had been tempted, sharing a long look that said a lot without uttering a word. Ryan was hot! But she declined and didn't think Kevin needed to hear about that, especially since she had considered saying yes. It was a moment of weakness when she and Kevin weren't getting along. The friendly flirting could have easily turned into something more. There's no doubt that Ryan was attractive and charming and she felt a strong pull, but didn't want to jeopardize the account. It wasn't her style to fool around with a client and she didn't want that to tarnish her reputation in the industry. However, Ryan was definitely a temptation.

Sensing her reluctance at the suggestion of a nightcap in her room, Ryan walked her to the hotel lobby and gave her

9

his charming smile, but she just smiled back and gave a little wave as she turned and headed toward the elevators. She told herself to not turn around and see if he was still there; that might break her resolve. As the elevator gave a classy ding, the doors slid open as she slipped inside without giving him a second glance. He was a client and she needed to keep it that way.

You'd think after several glasses of wine, she'd fall right into bed, but she was anxious and a little too wound up to sleep. She took off her make-up, applied her nighttime serums, moisturizer and eye cream, changed into old track shorts and a tank top before powering up her laptop to take care of her Inbox. Only 47 new emails since she logged off a few hours ago.

She found Dateline on TV, snuggled into the soft and cozy bright white sheets, and settled in for the night. Her flight was mid-afternoon the next day and she wasn't scheduled to visit Ryan's offices again, so she planned to sleep-in and enjoy a nice room service breakfast before heading to the airport.

Before she could get into the show, she heard a light knock at her door. With a curious look, she glanced at the clock, puzzled at who could be at the door so late.

"Who is it?" she called.

"It's me..." she heard the deep voice respond. Glancing through the peephole, she was surprised and somewhat excited as she opened the door.

"It's kind of late and I..."

"And you don't have an early flight, so why waste a night

on sleep…" Ryan asked, gently pushing down the straps on her tank top as he kicked the door shut with his foot.

"Well, when you put it like that," she murmured as his hands lightly traveled up and down her arms as she fell into bed with him.

CHAPTER 3

Arriving home on another Friday evening, Jillian dragged herself into the house, more tired than normal. She hoped she wasn't coming down with a cold. The air pressure combined with airline germs could easily get someone sick when you considered how much time she spent in the air. It might have been the extra-long night she'd had, she thought. She blushed a bit, remembering her spontaneous night with Ryan. She never even got to watch her Dateline. She shouldn't have done it, but thinking about it made her smile.

She dropped her bags in the entry and grabbed an orange juice from the kitchen, delaying saying hello to Kevin. They had a pretty big fight when she changed her return travel plans at the last minute. She had been scheduled to catch the Thursday flight, but switched it to Friday so she could finish her work without having to rush around too much. He didn't understand and accused her of just wanting to spend more time with Ryan, even though she continued to assure him that Ryan was just a client and nothing more. Yes, they had dinner a few times when she traveled, but that was so she didn't have to eat dinner alone every night on the road. Most nights, she dragged herself back to her hotel and ordered room service. Dinner out was a luxury when traveling for work. Most people thought she had time to see the sights and try all of the hotspots in whatever city she was in when, in reality, her trips consisted of visits to one boardroom after another and eating lunch from a box that the client ordered in, usually from Panera. It wasn't the glamorous travel that most people thought it was. Although there were also somewhat intimate dinners with Ryan, though all business, never responding to the sexual tension between them. Well, until recently, and that was a one-time thing, she reminded herself.

He definitely had to hear her come in. She made enough noise dropping her bags on the polished entry floor, but Kevin didn't appear. She knew he was home, having seen his car was in the garage. He must still be mad. It is going to be that kind of evening, she thought sourly, walking up the stairs to his office.

She noticed he hadn't looked at her when she walked in; hadn't taken his eyes off the screen to greet her. They hadn't seen each other since Sunday morning, before her flight, and this was the way he welcomed her home. Of course with Kevin, this behavior was more typical these days. When he was involved in something, there was no time for any "outside distractions" as he liked to call things he wasn't interested in at that precise moment.

Feeling slight rebuffed by the lack of affection on his part, she said, "Well, I guess I'll unpack and leave you to your work." Net sure if he even heard her, she glanced back at him before quietly leaving the room. I could probably have walked in naked, she thought, and he wouldn't have even noticed. Sometimes it irritated her that she didn't seem to be able to keep his attention anymore. It certainly wasn't from lack of trying, she thought with an angry shake of her head. Just a few weeks ago, he was happy to see her when she returned from a trip, but his jealousy of Ryan had increased, even though she continued to reassure him that nothing happened. Oh well, she's done babysitting his ego. It's his problem.

After unpacking from her trip, she quickly showered, changed into a worn pair of denim shorts and t-shirt. Grabbing a chilled wine cooler from the fridge and a glass of ice, she headed out to the patio and settled into a large chair and stretched her long, toned legs.

It was a lovely evening with a slight chill in the air, but the coolness was refreshing compared to the stale air of conference rooms and airplanes. Inhaling deeply, she glanced around at the neighboring townhouses. The neighborhood was nice, with professionals their age and some young families occupying the adjacent homes. She loved the area and quick commute to the office, but sometimes she missed the solitude of living alone in her simple one bedroom apartment. Plus, it could get a little noisy in the summer with the parties and cookouts that were frequent on the weekends. The community pool was often packed by noon on most weekends in the summer.

When she moved in with Kevin, she had loved the vitality of the community and the spacious townhouse. The exclusivity of the neighborhood attracted her, plus the amenities that came with that exclusivity, including a boyfriend she adored. Back then, they had shared cocktails on the back deck of their place or a neighbor's, laughing well into the night before heading upstairs to make love until dawn. Those evenings had started to dwindle as her travel schedule increased. She remembered being in those early days of love with Kevin with late weekend mornings cuddling in bed, drinking cappuccinos from his espresso machine and napping the afternoon away. Those were luxurious escapes from the workday grind and she missed

14

them, wondering when the last time was that they had shared a late morning in bed.

Before moving in with Kevin, she had lived in an old Victorian home that housed four large apartments, one on each floor. It was a mammoth of a house, a four-story mansion. Each apartment had a bedroom, bath, cozy kitchen, living room and a huge wraparound porch on the bottom floor that the tenants shared, along with the big backyard bordered from the neighbors with a towering wall of shrubbery. It was a great apartment and she'd fallen in love with it when she first crossed the threshold. Her apartment was on the first floor, with subtle gray walls and gleaming oak floors that were original to the house, she learned from the realtor. She loved the simplicity and added her personal stamp with her furnishings and décor, focusing on a comfortable palette that complimented the soft gray.

That's how she and Ann met. Ann lived in the apartment above hers. Kevin didn't really care for Ann and always seemed to find something that would "suddenly come up" and prevent her from visiting her friend. Another of his annoying character flaws, she thought, her irritation growing more and more. Maybe it was time to reevaluate their relationship, she thought. Maybe things weren't headed in the direction she planned. Then again, she wasn't exactly sure what she wanted. She thought that if they were living in a few decades earlier, he would have been the sole earner and would have wanted her to stay home and keep house. She shook her head thinking how unrealistic that was these days, but she's seen it happen.

"There you are," said Kevin, walking out onto the patio from the kitchen. "I was looking all over for you. What are you doing out here?" He asked while settling into the chair

15

next to her. He helped himself to her glass, proceeding to empty it.

Still annoyed with him for ignoring her before, she replied, "I'm just enjoying the quiet," and refilled her glass. "It's such a beautiful evening, do you want to light the fire pit and catch-up out here?"

"A fire? Now?" he asked, with a look of confusion. "You need to get a move on or we're going to be late. We don't have time for a fire tonight, Jillian." For the first time, she honed in on his wardrobe change. He was now wearing a pair of navy pants and a Williams Consulting golf shirt, both perfectly pressed.

"What are you talking about, Kevin?"

He signed dramatically; "Don't tell me you've forgotten our plans for the evening, Jillian? We made the arrangements weeks ago." Kevin the dramatic, as she had started to think of him, shook his head in a silent reprimand for her transgressions.

"What plans? My only plan was to relax after another week on the road," she said, adding a smile to ease the tension. She wasn't in the mood to fight.

"We have a cocktail reception with some clients, important clients who could bring a lot of business our way. We do have other clients to try to sign, not just Ryan, so I suggest you freshen up and change into something more appropriate than denim shorts and a t-shirt. Why don't you wear that red dress I bought you last week, unless you already wore it with another client this week?"

She slowly started to seethe at his reference to Ryan.

"Sorry, but I checked my calendar and there's nothing on it for tonight," she said, stretching her arms to work out some of the kinks. She thought about booking a massage soon as she looked again at Kevin, waiting for his next move. When had their relationship become such a battle of wits? It was becoming more and more like a tense game of chess, but no matter how she tired of it, she wasn't going to concede defeat. There was still a relationship to fight for, even as strained, as it might be these days.

"Well, obviously you dropped the ball on this and it's inconceivable to cancel, Jillian. They're clients," he reminded her in a condescending tone that she was finding more and more irritating. The breeze picked up a bit, sending wafting scents of a barbeque, making her hungry. Kevin was still talking business, but she was thinking about food.

"Anyway, we have to leave in 15 minutes if we're going to make it on time." With that, he rose and went into the house, leaving her alone again, to stew.

That was so typical of him, she thought. He was becoming pretty good at gaslighting her to make her think she was the crazy one, that she forgot an appointment. She had just spent the last several days traveling, spending her time in meetings during the day and client dinners during the evening. Granted, it was nice to wine and dine on the company's dime, but tonight she just wanted to relax. Enough is enough, she thought, but dutifully went into the house reminding herself that it was business and that came first. She'd have to have a serious discussion with Kevin and soon; she was tired of being his doormat.

Later that evening, she and Kevin were standing amidst a group of their co-workers. Including Kevin, all of the vice presidents were present, as was their CEO, Michael Williams, the brainchild and founder of Williams Consulting. He had such an energetic personality that even the most fickle employees found inspiration and excitement with the direction of the company under his leadership.

"Well, Jillian," Michael began, his voice deep and booming, "how as your trip this week? I understand you met with Ryan at Morton and his crew?"

Michael Williams was a no-nonsense leader who didn't like small talk or chitchat; he got right to the point and expected the same from others. He definitely didn't join the 3 o'clock coffee club in the office. When he asked a question, he expected a prompt, direct answer. Jillian kept this in mind as she quickly considered her answer.

"It went very well. Morton's board attended my final presentation and everyone seemed to be aligned with the proposal we made. I expect to pass them over to Kevin's group to sign their contract," she said with a glance at Kevin, who was across the room chatting with Alexis Kaufman, another client executive at Williams.

"Good, good," Michael praised, lightly touching her elbow while guiding her away from the rest of the group for a more private conversation. "I know I don't have to tell you how valuable you are to this organization and the work we do. Your experience and expertise have been advantageous as we continue to grow our business. You and Kevin make a great team. I see a very bright future for you here," he added, as he strolled over to another group of employees waiting for a minute of the charismatic leader's time.

She wondered what he meant by his last comment, but

didn't have time to dwell on it, as Kevin approached. They had basically made up in the car but she let him know she wasn't happy with how he treated her and they needed to have a talk. She hoped he wasn't planning to have that discussion now. His face was drawn tight and she wondered if he was still angry with her.

"Can I talk to you for a minute?" Kevin whispered in her ear, making her jump a little at the feel of his breath on her skin like a caress and she found herself shivering slightly in response to the intimacy of the moment. Regardless of what her powerful female mind was telling her, her body still physically responded to him.

Walking out on the balcony, away from the cocktail party that was in full swing. "Are you having a good time?" he inquired, still slightly scowling as he looked around at everything but her. What was wrong with him?

"I'm getting tired, Kevin. It's been a long week. How much longer do we have to stay?" To be honest, her mind was still processing Michael's comments about her future with the company. Was that a sign that she was going to get a promotion? She certainly felt she deserved to be recognized for her efforts and be promoted to the open director position more than anyone else on staff. But, she wasn't completely sure it was hers for the asking. Some alarm bells were going off in her head, warning her that something was going on, but she couldn't quite place her finger on it, and now Kevin wanted her time when all she wanted to do was go home and crawl into bed.

"We'll be leaving soon, but there's some unfinished business I think we need to address," he added while reaching into his jacket pocket and pulling out a small, blue Tiffany box.

Without a word, she simply stared at the box in his hand, unaware that several of their colleagues and clients had quietly followed them out to the balcony. She couldn't believe he was doing this. Was he proposing? It was too soon; surely he knew that! The way he treated her earlier, she thought they were headed for a breakup, not a lifelong commitment. Her eyes darted around, like a deer in headlights as her mind swirled, her stomach churning. She wasn't ready to settle down, she was too consumed with building her career. Everyone was looking at them, grinning with anticipation of her answer. She felt lightheaded as he got down on one knee, taking her left hand in his, "Jillian Simmons, will you marry me?" His earlier tension disappeared as his confident smile shone brightly as though there was so doubt at what her answer would be.

Suddenly, a round of applause exploded around them as everyone joined in the celebration. Toasts were made while Jillian stared in shock at Kevin who was still grinning with confidence. But it wasn't a celebration, she wanted to cry out. This wasn't supposed to be happening. She wasn't even supposed to be here tonight. She should have stayed home, relaxing and reading a good book. Sure, she loved Kevin, but the life they had begun to build together wasn't exactly on solid ground at the moment. She remembered how just moments ago, she saw him huddled with Alexis, looking at her as more than a co-worker. This wasn't the right time and definitely not the right place.

Glancing at him, her voice suddenly hoarse, she whispered, "Kevin, you really shouldn't have done this." He thought she meant splurging on Tiffany when she was referring to a surprise proposal. His confidence and arrogance had obviously not allowed for questions about what if she said no.

"Oh, come on, Jillian, everyone's anxious. Speak-up with your YES," he admonished, like she was a petulant schoolgirl. "Let me just slip this on your finger," he continued as the stunning pear-shaped diamond dazzled brightly. The ring felt cold and wrong on her finger. Kevin flashed his eyes on hers as she didn't immediately accept his proposal.

But instead of playing along, she flushed deeply, drew her hands away from his and walked back into the room, leaving him, his ring and their co-workers behind, blinking away the tears that threatened to fall. She wouldn't cry in front of them. She heard murmurings behind her, but the ringing in her ears was too loud to understand what they were saying, though she could guess. Her heart was beating wildly with horror at the scene that just took place. She left the building without a backward glance, the night air refreshing her as she called an Uber.

Her breathing was ragged as she collapsed in the backseat with her eyes closed and knots in her stomach. She tried to gulp in more air, feeling lightheaded as tears puddled in the corner of her eyes but she quickly pushed them back. What had she just one? She was confused and didn't understand why in the world Kevin would propose to her, after ignoring her at home earlier. They hadn't even discussed the subject of marriage privately and he goes and pops the question in front of their co-workers.

"Ugh," she groaned out load, giving the Uber driver a smile so he didn't think she was annoyed with his driving. "Sorry, it's been a long day," she said, thinking how humiliated Kevin must be, making the pit in her stomach even worse. She could still picture him there with the ring and a smile for the crowd gathered around them. Did someone take a picture, she wondered, remembering a flash? What a disaster the evening had become and there was nothing she could do about it. Unfortunately, knowing Kevin, he wouldn't understand where she was coming from and would sulk for days, maybe even weeks, considering the magnitude of the situation.

CHAPTER 4

Kevin didn't come home that night and she didn't know what message he was trying to send her. After all, they live in his house, not hers. She was certain he hadn't come home because she had been up most of the night tossing and turning, unable to escape the replay of the scene from the previous night. It was like a bad Lifetime movie that wouldn't end! She could see him, smiling at her like there was a joke she didn't know about, with the signature blue box in his hands, waiting for the moment before they let out a loud cheer, but the cheer never came, just stunned whispers and phone flashes. She had walked out on him and she was sure there'd be no way to make up for that. He'd been humiliated and embarrassed, two things Kevin never forgave. But, it wasn't like it was her fault! They'd never discussed marriage and if they had, he'd have known she wasn't ready to make that kind of commitment at this stage in her life. She didn't think she was too young for marriage; it was more complex than that. She didn't want to give-up the time and attention she devoted to her job, plus she wasn't sure that she wanted to marry Kevin, truth be told.

Sipping the cappuccino that she brewed on the complicated espresso maker, she thought about how their relationship wasn't that stable. She suspected he wasn't faithful to her, but didn't have definite proof to backup her suspicions. It was just a gut feeling, though her gut hadn't been wrong that often. And of course, she had spent the night, only one night, with Ryan after a night of a lot of wine and even more built-up sexual tension.

Looking around, she realized that he really hadn't been home; the house was exactly as she'd left it the night before. Damn him, she thought, stepping into the shower! Why did he have make a personal moment so public in front of their co-workers, not to mention a few of their clients? That wasn't a moment to be shared with virtual strangers. In her mind, the perfect proposal was a private affair with the couple in a romantic setting, maybe a picnic or intimate candlelight dinner. It was such a cliché, but that was her dream. She pictured two people in love, with eyes only for each other, unaware of their surroundings even in a crowd. Their love and desire would block out everything around them, as if they were in a private world to which only they had the key. With a shake of her head and a thorough rinse of her conditioner, she laughed to herself. Things like that just don't happen in the real world.

Kevin's townhouse was less than ten minutes away. Jillian enjoyed the easy drive, opting to take a weave of back roads that reminded her of her hometown. But she still loved the look of the gorgeous city skyline with tall buildings that reflected the rising sun.

The office was quiet when she walked in and she wondered if everyone knew what had happened the previous night. Of course they did, she chided herself. Gossip that good was never kept under wraps! It's already spread like wildfire, she thought, as she made her way to her office on the other side of the building.

The corporate office of Williams Consulting was located in a new three-story building constructed in a growing, thriving business park near the city. They occupied the first floor of the modern glass and steel structure and had an option on the still empty second floor, if the company's growth continued. Adjacent to the heavily trafficked four-lane interstate, the area had become a popular residence for companies beginning to ease out of the downtown rat race with daily traffic tension and construction delays. These days, some highway or main thoroughfare was always under construction.

The business park was a good choice in real estate because of its convenient location. Over the past decade, the suburbs expanded out of the shrinking metropolitan areas with more skyscrapers than skylights. Jillian thought about her days working in the city. Summer days were nice, but those cold winter days when the gusts of wind from the river swirled between the skyscrapers were just too much.

Surrounded on one side by a ritzy townhouse complex with at least one hundred units and more being built for the new young professionals and active retirees, the business park boasted two championship golf courses, two hotels, several restaurants, shops and service businesses including a dry cleaner, laundry service and grocery store that delivered. Not to mention the other regional, national and international corporations that call the area home. It was a prominent, growing community with several buildings awarded for their commitment to the environment that were also a short distance to the city. Most of the occupants worked for the companies that leased their office space in the same community, making short commutes and an almost small-town feeling. Well, a small-town feeling where housing cost well over any small town she'd lived in.

Her office was a small space towards the back of the building where the other client executives, sales representatives and a few secretaries were located. It was a small space with just enough room for her L-shaped desk, credenza and two guest chairs that faced her desk. The window afforded a gorgeous view of the tenth hole of one of the golf courses and the well-tended landscape beyond. In the summer, she added pots of bright and colorful flowers for a pop of color.

Stepping into the room, her heels quietly sinking into the carpet, she removed her laptop from her bag and plugged it in, while stowing her purse into a desk drawer. She spent a minute gazing out at the golf course to quell her anxiety while her laptop booted up. Turning around, she entered her username and password, surprised when a flashing message told her that her username and password were incorrect. She retyped them and waited, confusion filling her face as the same incorrect login message displayed again. Reaching for the phone to call the help desk, she paused as their department secretary stopped in her doorway.

"Oh, good morning, Betty," she addressed the older woman with a smile. "I can't seem to login in this morning, is the network down?"

"I think the network is running," Betty replied, and then added after a brief pause, "John wants to see you, Jillian." She was referring to the company's HR manager. Without looking Jillian in the eye, she stood there are waited as the younger woman rose from her desk and walked to the door.

As a nervous feeling started in the pit of her stomach,

Jillian asked, "Do you know what he wants? Are we already interviewing for the new sales position? I haven't finished reading the resumes we received for the job, yet." They were desperately in need of another, perhaps two additional sales reps thanks to the recent growth spurt their western push yielded. Or, she thought maybe he wants to discuss the promotion she was in contention for. There were a few inside candidates, but she was clearly the one with the most experience and qualifications for the job. She had several new ideas that she had discussed with Kevin, seeking his advice on changes and new programs to implement. The promotion would be a great addition to her LinkedIn profile, one step away from vice president, at such a young age. The promotion would make her the youngest manager at Williams Consulting. Maybe that's what Michael Williams meant last night when he mentioned her bright future. But did last night change everything? Surely their personal lives wouldn't hurt her career, she considered as a warm flushed started at her head and worked its way down to her toes.

"I'm not sure what he wants to talk about," said Betty, her glance not quite reaching Jillian's eyes as she became suddenly busy with her computer.

Jillian convinced herself she was going to be promoted, but as she glanced in Kevin's office on her way to HR, she saw Kevin and Michael Williams in a heated debate that fell silent as they noticed her walking past. Given Michael's warm reception last evening, she was a little unnerved at the chill she suddenly felt from him. Feeling completely unwelcome, she offered a slight smile, and then continued on her path while neither man smiled or offered any kind of greeting. That nauseous feeling hit her like a kick to the gut as she made her way to HR.

Could this meeting really have something to do with what happened last night? How in the world could her refusal of Kevin's marriage proposal affect her job, she thought as she reached John's door. No, she told herself, that's ridiculous. But, as she pushed open the door, the serious look on John's face told her that whatever the meeting was about, it wasn't good. She cleared her throat and greeted him with a smile, feeling her confidence creeping in. John was a few years older than Jillian, with dark brown hair going gray at the temples and brown eyes. They had become friends during their time together at Williams, often doing happy hour when she was in town. That happened less frequently after she started dating Kevin. Looking at him now, sensing his dismay, really made her feel nostalgic and miss something she hadn't realized had been gone. She'd been so wrapped up in Kevin, that it was easy to let her old friends slip away.

"Good morning, Jillian, thanks for dropping by," he said as he stood to shake her hand and close his office door. He gestured to her to take one of the guest chairs as he returned to his chair, effectively putting the desk between them, making sure she understood this was a business meeting.

"I didn't drop by, you asked to see me. Betty said you wanted to see me," she corrected herself, crossing her legs as she perched on the edge of the chair. She felt a little uncomfortable, but told herself to calm down and mentally counted to ten, a trick she used when her nerves threatened to engulf her. It's nothing, she told herself and added a confident smile when John glanced in her direction.

"Yes, that's right," he began, clearing his throat and shuffling through some papers on his desk. "Jillian, we need to talk. I'm afraid we have a bit of a problem."

"Problem?" she asked as her mind went into work-mode, thinking of the strategy she would use to fix the client's problem, but quickly remembered this wasn't a client meeting.

"Let me get straight to the point, Jillian," he paused, thinking of the right words to use, tapping his finger on the desk as he cleared his throat. "We're going to have to let you go." This wasn't a position he liked to be in. Sure, he was used to firing people; it was part of his job and a way of life in HR, but that didn't mean he liked doing it. Especially when he really liked the person he was letting go and didn't agree with the decision. He liked Jillian. She was a likeable person and an asset to their organization He couldn't refuse the task he'd been given, but that didn't mean he had to like it.

Michael Williams contacted him this morning and told him in no uncertain terms, that Jillian was to be relieved of her duties immediately and escorted from the building no later than noon today. When he had asked why, Michael mentioned they had received complaints from some of her clients who were threatening to pull their business if she wasn't replaced. John didn't believe that for a second, but Michael was the boss. However, John was at the previous night's cocktail reception and figured Kevin was behind the so-called complaints. He felt sorry for the lovely young lady seated in front of him, clearly upset by the blow he had just delivered to her, but it was out of his hands. He was just the messenger. In his opinion, the one who should be let go is Kevin McBride. The man was worthless, as far as business was concerned, but he was quite the player when it came to the ladies and socializing. He was certain Jillian was unaware of his extra-curricular activities when she traveled, but that wasn't his business. He had a feeling the conversation he and Jillian were about to have would put an end to her love for Mr. McBride.

"I'm sorry, John," she stammered, her voice rising an octave, "I don't understand what you're telling me. I'm being fired? Why am I being fired? Why?" though as soon as the words were out of her mouth, she knew the reason and was instantly enraged. "Don't tell me this is because of what happened last night with Kevin? John, is that what this is?" She jumped out of her seat, startling John.

"Now Jillian," he continued in a hurried voice, he didn't want to make a bad situation worse, but she was already gone from his office, striding back to her department with a head of steam.

Walking back to her office, her auburn hair swirling around her shoulders, she tried to maintain her composure and act like a professional while every bone in her body was screaming out at the injustice she had just been dealt. Well, if they wanted to let her go because of something in her personal life that was fine with her. She didn't want to work for a company that operated like that.

She reached Kevin's office, fully intending to give him a piece of her mind, after she gave him an opportunity to explain himself. She was secretly hoping that he would deny all knowledge and that there was another explanation for what was happening. In fact, this is the kind of situation she wouldn't believe it was part of an April Fools' Day joke! It was just too ludicrous to imagine that she had just been fired for turning down a marriage proposal she wasn't sure she wanted anyway. She had too much work to do. But, as she discovered, his office was dark and his laptop was done.

"Jillian, wait," called Alexis Cronwell, a coworker on her way back to her office. "Whatever happened?" The petite blonde asked in her breathy voice, her blue eyes bright with excitement. There was nothing Alexis liked better than office gossip. Grabbing her arm, she pulled Jillian into an empty conference room and shut the door behind her. "I heard what happened, but still can't believe it! You turned down Kevin's proposal?" The sugary return of her southern accent grated it on Julian's nerves like nails scratching down a chalkboard, because it was as fake as some other parts of Alexis.

"Come on, Jillian, you can tell me. Is it true?" This discussion and Alexis's reaction were all the talk to nearly send Jillian over the edge.

Head throbbing, locked in the conference room with Alexis was the last place she wanted to be right now. She didn't trust the other woman any more than she believed the blonde hair Alexis sported was natural. Then again, she knew what would happen after last night. In fact, Jillian wouldn't be surprised if rumors are circulating about her being fired less than five minutes ago. The office rumor mill had more strength than herd of cattle, she thought.

"I'm going to be late for a conference call," she informed Alexis, brushing past her. Turning to glance over her shoulder she added, "but yes, I did turn down Kevin's proposal."

Somewhat deflated and irritated by the confrontation with Alexis, she returned to her office. Seconds later, Betty appeared in her doorway once again, ringing her hands like a nervous mother.

"Jillian," she began, "I am so sorry for what happened. It's not going to be the same around here without you. Is there something you can do about this? We don't want to lose you!"

"Thanks, Betty, but it seems as though the powers that be have their minds made up, "she answered in a small voice, her bravado deflated in Betty's presence. The reality that she was now jobless, and of course homeless, was hitting her like a ton of bricks. It felt like the wind had been knocked out of her as she dropped into her desk chair, too dizzy and confused to focus on much of anything.

"I don't want to rush you, but I'm afraid I have to escort you from the building," Betty added in a regretful tone.

Jillian looked at her in disbelief, dumbfounded at what was happening. Silently she looked around her, wondering what to take and what to leave. There was just so much stuff crammed in her small office that it would take her hours to weed through everything. Plus, she didn't know where to put everything. She didn't have her own home to go to and she wasn't going to spend any more time than necessary at Kevin's house. But where would she go? All of her belongings might fit into her SUV and some stuff she could add to the storage space she rented for her furniture after moving in with Kevin. It was just much too confusing right now. Then she noticed the empty packing boxes sitting on the guest chairs in front of her desk.

"It's going to take me a few hours to go through everything, Betty" she said, rising and walking to her office door where the secretary stood with worry. "Give me two hours and I'll call you when I'm done."

Without an argument, the older woman retreated through

the doorway, allowing Jillian to close the door. She turned the lock and then sank back in her chair where she closed her eyes. She wouldn't cry; that was for certain. She would not allow herself to submit to the tears that threatened to overflow. She could cry later, but not now.

Leaving the office was a humiliating experience, but she managed to maintain a sense of dignity and pride with her head held high as she walked out of the building. In the end, she left with two boxes full of plants and a few travel mementos. She had uploaded some of her documents to the cloud, thinking it was a good idea to take them, but making sure she didn't break her NDA. You never know what the future will hold. Today was certainly proof of that.

All in all, she was exhausted physically, mentally and emotionally by the time she drove out of the parking lot. Betty followed her out and embraced her as she said goodbye, placing a soft kiss on her cheek. They were tears in her eyes as Jillian closed the car door, knowing things weren't going to get better until they got worse. She eased her car into traffic and headed out of the parking lot, not sure where to go.

She wanted nothing more than to go home, crawl back in bed and shut the world out for a few hours, but instead drove around for a bit before finally heading to the home she shared with Kevin, knowing she had to deal with him. Planning to confront him and pack her belongings, she cursed herself for moving in with him against her better judgment. Things having been off between them for a while, but she didn't realize how bad they'd gotten. Being out of town and away from the situation had blinded her to his unfortunate personality traits. Even though they shared domestic space, they really had a long-distance relationship. Other than weekends that were usually jam-packed with errands, unpacking, laundry and re-packing, they essentially lived in different cities most of the time. She would leave Sunday with one itinerary and destination and he with another or to the office until his next trip. It was a crazy life that had worked for them once upon a time and she wondered how it had all become so involved and bizarre. In a way, she was sad to be losing Kevin. However, the possibility of continuing their relationship was impossible. He'd hurt her too badly and she was so confused. He'd instigated her firing because of personal reasons. That was unforgivable as far as she was concerned. Her willpower to not break down was a surprise, even to herself. All she wanted to do was cry her heart out at the injustice of it all. It wasn't time for that now. In a few hours, maybe she would indulge, but not now. And after her refusal last night he'd never forgive her. Why did she feel like the bad guy? That was the unfair part of it all.

Letting herself in the front door, she paused to look around for the last time with the place she called home and wondered how she could ever have been comfortable in the cold, sterile surroundings. Their decorating tastes definitely differed, but he had been adamant about not allowing her to make any changes or add any creative touches her represented her style.

"This place and the renovations cost me a small fortune, Jillian, and I'm not going to change them. That's my final decision," he'd firmly said when she broached the subject a month after moving in with him. She hadn't brought it up again. In Kevin's mind, what he said was not to be questioned. She hadn't liked that thinking then and certainly didn't like it now. He thought that he could stand behind her and someone else's life because he felt like it.

Well that was a bunch of crap, she thought. Why did she put up with it for so long?

As she thought about it, the only real luxury she would miss would be the wildly expensive espresso machine he'd splurged on.

Hearing noises, she followed the sounds to Kevin's office. The door was slightly ajar and the lights were dim but that's where the sounds were coming from. Using the door open for a better look, she was shocked to find Kevin and Alexis sharing a very passionate kiss. Both jumped when they heard her gasp. In shock, she ran down the hall to the bedroom she and Kevin shared, locking the door behind her. With trembling hands, she went in her closet and tossed her suitcases on the bed. Racing around the room, she haphazardly threw things in her suitcases, not caring if they were folded or not. She grabbed jewelry and makeup, anything she could grab. With a glance at the bed, she wondered how many times Alexis had slept in her place while she was out of town. Or as was the case today, while she was at work and Kevin was at was at an "offsite meeting."

Twenty minutes later, with most of her belongings packed, she walked from the house without ever turning around to acknowledge either of them. Kevin followed her to the bedroom, beating on the door, asking for a chance to explain. She turned a deaf ear and didn't have any desire to hear anything he might have to say, remembering how cold he treated her when she refused his proposal last night. Any words out of his mouth, she now knew were nothing but lies.

CHAPTER 5

After pulling her car out of the driveway, she turned onto the highway and drove away. She didn't know where she was going or what she was going to do, but she knew that she couldn't stand to look at Kevin or Alexis. Both of them betrayed her. She expected it from Alexis, but it was Kevin's betrayal that hurt her the most. They had been lovers, a relationship that should've meant more to him than it obviously did. She felt as if the wind had been knocked out of her. And, now she forgave herself for her one night-stand with Ryan. Clearly, Kevin and Alexis had more than one night together in the past.

It was all just so terrible she thought. Glancing down at the steering wheel as a traffic rush past her, she realized that her hands were shaking. In fact, her whole body was trembling. But was it from hurt or anger? The events of the morning took their toll on her emotionally, mentally and now physically. It was more than she could bear. Looking around her, tears streaming down her face, she pulled into the gas station on the right and turned her car off. Wiping the tears from her cheeks, unable to stop the flow of them she fumbled in her purse for her cell phone and dialed Ann.

She didn't know what to do, where to go, but Ann would listen to her. She needed to clear her head and figure out her next step. She couldn't sit in the gas station parking lot all day.

"This is Ann," the friendly voice greeted her after she dialed the number.

"Ann..." Jillian sobbed into the phone. Just hearing her friend's voice brought on a new set of tears, melting what was left of her make up. Hearing her friend's kind voice was enough to make her cry again

"Jilly?" Ann questioned, shocked at the sound of her friend's voice. "Are you crying? What's the matter? Where are you?" She glanced around not wanting her coworkers to overhear her conversation she closed her office door and switched from speakerphone to her Bluetooth headset.

"Oh Ann," Jillian sniffed, "I don't know what to do...I, uh," she blew her nose, "I was just fired, I turned down Kevin's very public marriage proposal and I just...I just found out that he's been cheating on me," she finished in a loud cry. It wasn't like her to fall apart so easily. Usually Jillian was a strong person, but she could only handle so much in one day. Usually she was the supportive person lending her shoulder to someone else to cry on, but today she needed to take comfort, not give it. Taking a deep breath, she wiped her eyes and tried to regain her composure. Ann was her closest friend and she needed a friend right now; she knew she was on the verge of losing control. She needed Ann to help put her back together. This was like a bad episode of Sex and the City, when Carrie and Big broke-up and Carrie cried on Miranda's shoulder. She had this thought, taking a deep breath and slightly chuckling to herself.

"Are you still there?" Ann asked worried about her friend who was still crying into the phone. "What do you mean you got fired? Why? Did you say Kevin's been having an affair and proposed to you; that sounds complicated!"

"I was fired and asked to leave the building with all of my belongings because of some, quote unquote, complaints that some of our clients had made about me. But I know that's not the truth. I know that's not why I was fired. As sure as I'm sitting here, it was because of what happened with Kevin last night," anger starting to replace sadness as she said it out loud. The tears had stopped falling, but her nose was stuffy and she could feel a terrible headache behind her right eye as her head began to throb. She was certain that her face was a puffy, blotchy, red mess, but she didn't care.

"What?!" Ann nearly screeched into the phone, "what do you mean Kevin's marriage proposal? I don't understand."

Jillian told her the whole story from start to finish not leaving out any of the details. Ann listened intently, not asking any questions or making comments until Jillian had finished. It felt good to talk about it, though the events were still so surreal, as if it had happened to someone else and not her.

"Ann, I'm headed to the spa for the weekend," she decided in that instant, "I need to get away and clear my head. I just," she paused, taking a deep breath, "I just don't know what to do now. I mean, my car is loaded down with my stuff that I took from Kevin's. Clothes, plants, files, mail, books, all of the stuff that I could grab after seeing him and Alexis. Oh, it was just so terrible," she ended, gripping the steering wheel tighter. She was still parked at the gas station. A light, steady rain had started to fall, blurring the windshield.

"I have an idea," she said more cheerfully than she really felt, "why don't you join me there tonight? I'm going to schedule as many treatments as I can and would love the company. If I go alone, I'll just sit and cry and I really don't want to do that. By tomorrow afternoon, I'll be ready to climb the walls. But, if you come along, it could be fun. We could get massages and facials and soak in the whirlpool. What do you say? I'll call and book us a suite and you can come up after work tonight."

CHAPTER 6

After stowing most of her belongings in the storage space she was already renting, she tucked her Kate Spade cosmetic case and matching overnight bag she unearthed from storage in the trunk and left the rest as it was. Her calmness was surprising as she thought about the life-changing events she'd just been forced to accept. After a few deep, cleansing breaths, she reminded herself to take it one day at a time.

Still low in miles because she hardly drove it due to her work travel, the SUV was an extravagance she allowed herself after accepting the job with Williams Consulting (and the large bonus that was part of her hiring bonus.) She had negotiated for this job, unlike in the past when she'd been too timid to discuss money in her previous positions. Usually, she took whatever salary was offered so she didn't seem demanding, when in fact, she had accepted jobs for far less than what she was really worth. This time, she had been so forthright and determined that her employment deal included company stock options and quarterly bonuses based on pre-determined objectives. All in all, she had been quite proud of her accomplishments and had rewarded herself with a top-of-the-line new silver SUV, accompanied by a smooth leather interior and every customization available. It was a wonderful ride and she loved driving it. Kevin preferred his sleek, black sports car, but she relished sitting up high in the sporty, all-purpose vehicle. Since it was a Mercedes, luxury wasn't an upgrade, it was more of a given.

One phone call later and she was on her way to her favorite resort and spa located an hour and a half away, nestled in the neighboring mountain range. Once cleared of the city traffic and the rain, she set the cruise control, turned the radio on and let the scenery sooth her. The leaves of the trees were a breathtaking palette of varying shades of green. She could smell early summer in the air. There was something about the hint of the warm weather to come that brought out the kid in her. It calmed her, reminding her of the exhilaration of her childhood – something that Jillian needed right now.

Ann was meeting her there that evening, so she booked a two-bedroom suite in the main building. The property included a variety of accommodations, including townhouses, larger private homes, cottages, a rustic lodge and the new luxurious chateau with six floors of rooms, suites and magnificent penthouses. In addition, there was a PGA golf course, several ski slopes and an outdoor fireplace. However, Jillian was more interested in the wine cellar and spa during this visit.

Jillian's visit to the spa thoroughly refreshed her. Two days later, she left the spa feeling more refreshed and in control of her emotions. She had enjoyed the whole experience, even though she was still broken- hearted and unemployed. She spared no expense in her mission to attempt to wash away the events of the past few days. It was hard to believe how much her life had changed in less than one week.

The time away from the real world was not only energizing for her physically, but also mentally and emotionally. There was little conversation during her spa treatments and the silence was welcome after so much conversation and noise had filled the past several years of her life. Being alone with her thoughts was a good thing. She cried her heart out until she was out of tears and she vowed to push Kevin and Williams Consulting out of her mind. Most people would be bitter and angry over what had happened, and she was no exception. But it was almost exhausting to carry so much anger in her, and it certainly wasn't going to do any good, so she tried her best to not dwell on it.

Instead, she recalled memories of her childhood, when life seemed to be so much easier, with fewer decisions to make. When she was little, life was full of routines planned for you by someone else. She woke up, got dressed, had breakfast, went to school, came home from school, had dinner, played with her sister until bath and bedtime, with the whole cycle repeating itself day in and day out. Of course, as she got older, the routine had matured with her. Even though it was nearly the same every day, it was comforting and had reassured that her childhood was good.

She and her sister, Jessica, had played with the neighborhood kids from morning until night each and every day swimming, riding bikes, playing hide and seek until the sun went down. Anything that didn't include schoolwork was fine with them. They were glorious years to remember and cherish, especially when they pulled out the old home movies their dad had recorded.

Jessica's children enjoyed watching the movies too and laughed at the "old" hairdos and clothes the Simmons sisters had sported in the "olden days." These movies were a way for her to remember the happy childhood with her father, who had had a heart attack when she was in high school.

A junior engrossed with her homework, clubs and her boyfriend, she had been speechless when the counselor had called her to her office where her mom waited to break the news to her and Jessica. The sisters had been nervous, both suspecting bad news, but hoping otherwise. Too stunned to speak at the time, Jillian remembered sitting there in disbelief, sure that the counselor had called the wrong person to the office. It wasn't their dad who had died, it was someone else's, and they would attend the funeral of a friend's dad, not receive and greet visitors at their father's funeral. Tears still came to her eyes when she thought of her kind, fun, loving, gentle father who had been robbed of so much of his life. He died at a young age, forever deprived of watching his girls grow into the bright, educated, loving women he'd raised with their mother. Their children wouldn't have anyone to call Grandpa.

Even with the sad memories running through her mind, it felt good to remember the past as she looked toward her future. So much so, in fact, that after leaving the spa as a new woman, she called her mother to let her know she was coming home for a visit. Not wanting to tell her mother what had happened recently on the telephone, she made up an excuse of taking a few days off.

It had been too long since she'd visited home. She regularly talked to her mom and texted her sister, as well as her brother-in-law, Jack, and her nieces and nephews, Daniel and Hannah. A few days with them in person would do her good. She and Jessica could take long walks while Jillian told her everything that had happened. Their relationship far surpassed sisterhood. It had been a long time since they'd taken the time to really catch-up in person.

They were the best of friends and confided in one another without censoring details. She felt better about going home and facing her family after talking everything over with Ann. As she heard the story with her own ears, she knew that it wasn't her fault. That alone was reassuring, but the uncertainty of the future didn't make anything much better.

CHAPTER 7

With a contemplative expression, Matt Parker studied the blueprints lying on the expansive desk in his sunlit office. They were the plans for a new family room addition he was starting work on tomorrow. He wanted to look everything over one last time before his crew started the prep work. He'd talked to his project manager already to make sure the worksite had all of the supplies they'd need to start the demo.

The homeowners had been more than thrilled with the design he'd worked up for them and were anxious to see the final results, though that was still a few weeks, a lot of sweat and hard work away. The plans called for one large room with a cathedral ceiling hosting skylights and ceiling fans, a stone hearth and fireplace built into one corner of the room, floor to ceiling doors and windows on three sides and an outside deck that surrounded the structure on three sides. The view beyond was of the large lake where real estate was prime and pricey. But the couple he was working for had bought the property before the town had realized the full draw and potential of the waterfront area. It had been a smart investment for them, and Matt was just as excited about the project as they were. The end result would be worth the wait, he had promised them when they had expressed their impatience at where they stood on his long waiting list. His construction company was in great demand year-round, but mostly during the warm months when the remodeling bug seemed to bite everyone at the same time. Cold months were for inside jobs, but the summer months were when outdoor construction was king.

With a final glance at the design, he rolled the plans into the cardboard tube, where they would stay until tomorrow morning. Turning off the desk lamp, he made his way to the door and locked up for the night. More often than not, he spent more time in this room than in his house. Most days, his work didn't end until well into the evening; long after his crew was already home with their families, enjoying dinner, a game of tag with their kids before nightfall or holding up the bar at the local watering hole frequented by the laborers in the area. A childless bachelor, his work was his life, as well as his passion and he was good at it. There was a sense of satisfaction that could be gained after a long, hard day of working with your hands, building something. Taking a drawing that only existed on paper and working it, molding and shaping it until the final product reflected the details of the design plan. That's what he did for a living. Taking others dreams and making them reality was one way of thinking about his chosen profession. Actually, the profession chose him as much as he chose it.

Even as a child, Matt knew that he wanted to build things. His favorite toys grew as he did. He started with building blocks then Lincoln Logs and onto Legos. At a young age, he had built fairly impressive structures and always began with a design on paper, starting with crayons and art paper, and then advancing to a drawing board and more professional materials. But he didn't just want to sit behind a desk and draw the designs; he wanted to be involved in the construction process as well so he could see his drawings come to life.

After just one semester of college, he left the academic world in pursuit of an apprenticeship where he learned the tricks of his trade. Seemingly oblivious to the long, exhausting hours, he worked hard to learn as much as he could. He shadowed other contractors until he felt confident that he was ready to step out on his own. Though his parents weren't there to watch as their only son started a successful business from the bottom up, he felt their approval of his career choice. They had been the ones to push him into attending college. He hadn't wanted to go, but did so out of respect for the loving parents who had raised him and his sister. They were killed in a violent car crash when he and his sister were just out of high school. From then on, they were on their own. Figuring it was a waste of time and money, he only lasted the four short months before walking away from it forever. From that point on, he never looked back or regretted his decision. He took a few design courses online for preparing final plans, but he always started sketching out on his large drafting table with paper and pencil.

He set the security alarm, locked the door and climbed into his old pickup truck. The ride home was a short one and he liked that. His brother-in-law drove an hour each way to work and hated it. He frequently said the drive was enough to make him crazy some days. Matt was glad he didn't have a long commute; his days were long enough just from the time he spent working. Putting on his aviator sunglasses, he pulled into traffic as the sun was dipping out of view under a passing cloud.

CHAPTER 8

When he got home, the message light on his answering machine was blinking. Punching the play button on the machine, he wandered over to the wet bar in the comer of the living room and grabbed a cold beer from the fridge. Shrugging out of his shirt, he stood facing the French doors, enjoying the view of the lake out his window. The breeze drifting in had a slight chill that was welcome after a long day of work.

Stretching his arms high above his head, he flexed and relaxed his muscles, trying to loosen the kinks from a long, hard day of work. At just over six feet tall, he was a strong man with firm muscles earned from hard work and an unrelenting schedule. Most days, he worked twelve hours, if not more. It was a crazy life, but he loved it. His body certainly showed the effects of his career. His skin was tanned golden bronze from the days spent in the sun working side-by-side with his crew, as he liked to do when he wasn't on sales calls or managing the business. He was glad he added a project manager to his workforce so he wasn't visiting multiple worksites every day.

His dark brown hair was a little long and hung just over the collar of his shirt. Maybe this weekend he'd get a haircut, he thought, as he ran a large, strong hand over the dark stubble of his chin that had been smooth earlier in the day. He had to shave every day or deal with the inevitable five o'clock stubble that sprouted throughout the day. All in all, with his deep blue eyes, Matt Parker was a very good-looking man and quite the eligible bachelor around town. He was the kind of man who got second glances, even after he'd started walking away. Many women had tried to catch him, but he managed to escape their traps for years and had no intention of settling down yet, much to his sister's dismay. She wanted him to find someone to make him happy and to marry. Even though he continually told her he wasn't interested, that he just hadn't found the right person and was too busy building his business, she still bothered him about finding someone. He had found love once upon a time, but it hadn't worked out.

The first message began playing, "Matt, it's Susan." He figured his sister would be one of the callers. Though only separated by a year, she tried to mother him. But as the gestures would annoy some men his age, he just smiled and appreciated the close relationship their parents had instilled in them when were younger. "I just wanted to let you know that I left a small meatloaf with potatoes and carrots in your oven. It should still be warm, but you can heat it in the microwave if it's not." He smiled and shook his head at her.

Once or twice a week he would come home from work and find one of Susan's dinners waiting for him in her crockpot on the counter. They joked that she was his part-time Grub Hub delivery service. He appreciated the meals, especially since his sister was an excellent cook.

The second message began playing. "Hey, Matt, it's Jack. Just wanted to let you know that softball practice was moved back an hour, so we'll see you at the field tomorrow night at 7:30."

The softball team was his one indulgence in a hobby. His work left little time for outside interferences, which could make for a lonely life, but it had also made him a successful businessman. He didn't have time for a wife, or even a girlfriend, for that matter, though several had tried. It wasn't like he was a monk or a boy scout, he just had priorities, and a steady girlfriend didn't fit into them right now. Sure, he dated, but nobody ever got too close and he rarely brought women back to his house. Lately, he had been seeing someone with more frequency than usual, but it wasn't headed anywhere permanent. She was fun and good companionship, not to mention pretty entertaining in the bedroom, but neither had been interested in anything more serious than that. It was a good fit for both of them. Though he was beginning to sense that she wanted to take it to another level, and he wasn't sure he wanted that.

The softball team allowed him to unwind and relax with his friends. Most of the guys on the team had known one another all their lives, having gone to school together. Back in high school, Matt had played on the baseball team, where he'd been MVP more than any student in the school's history. He was a good leader and player, and an even better hitter, who broke school records and set a few new ones back in the day. Matt was still a good player, but he saw the game differently now than he had then. Now, it was fun and relaxing and didn't mean as much as it had in high school. He was still competitive, but not like he used to be.

While his dinner heated, he wandered out to the deck that ran the length of his house. The deck was only a few feet off of the ground, but high enough so that you were elevated above the backyard. He added steps off of both ends that led to the expansive yard below. Hiring a professional landscaper had been a worthwhile investment since he didn't know a perennial from an annual to save his life. Plus, he wanted plants that would blend in with what was already there and were simple, requiring little maintenance on his part. That's exactly what he got in the natural line of trees that bordered his yard on both sides of his property. Scattered throughout the rest of the yard, the oak trees provided ample shade, but didn't interfere with his view of the lake and his small beach area. Calling the small area a beach was a stretch of the imagination, but where his yard ended, a stretch of sandy terrain extended into the lake where the water was shallow. The entire space was only about twenty by thirty feet. Though it wasn't large enough or deep enough for a boat, he had a modest dock and planned on adding some seating where you could fully appreciate the prime real estate.

Like the homeowners of the renovation project he was starting the following day, he had also bought his house and property before the lake area had experienced a real estate boom. His clients lived on the other side of the lake that was developed several years ago. His house was only ten years old, but had a rustic feel that made you believe it had been there as long as the lake had. Over time, he had expanded the house and property until he was satisfied with the finished product. The outcome was a handsome home with lots of light and detailed woodwork throughout. Word of mouth had spread about the magnificent job he'd done on his own home in his limited spare time, bringing him more residential clients than ever.

CHAPTER 9

No matter how old you are, no matter what kind of job you do; if you're a successful, powerful attorney or a cashier at a small grocery store, nothing can replace the feeling you have when coming home after a long absence. Thinking back, it had been over a year since Jillian had driven these familiar streets that she could probably drive with her eyes closed, allowing memory and instinct to lead the way. These were the streets where she had learned to drive. Her father had exercised such patience during those days, especially when she'd been learning to parallel park. She had lost count of the number of times her father had cringed as the tires bounced against the curb yet again. Smiling at the memory, she was glad to be home.

Though it had been a long time since her last visit, not much had changed in her mom's neighborhood. The houses looked the same, maybe a few new coats of paint to freshen things up, but for the most part, she knew what to expect to see in each of the yards on her block. There was comfort in the familiar, she thought with a smile. Her mom and sister had visited her when she wasn't traveling a couple of times a year, but it just wasn't the same. Plus, Kevin hadn't been overly thrilled at having houseguests. As a result, their last visit had been short and uncomfortable. Shaking her head, she pushed the incident from her mind, not wanting to dwell on the bad memory or Kevin.

Seeing the neighboring houses, remembering the friends she had played with when she was younger added some long overdue nostalgia.

Walking up the front steps to the house she had called home for so many years gave her a warm feeling. The porch swing and colorful flowers on every surface available were so familiar, she was almost overwhelmed by the comfort of coming home. But it wasn't until the front door opened with a slight creak that her emotions got the best of her. Her chest tightened as she saw her mom standing on the other side of the screen door, hair pulled back into a loose ponytail, a few strands of the dark brown curls that resembled her own, minus the strands of gray, escaping and falling loosely around her face. Her mother was an attractive woman with green eyes and a petite figure she maintained through daily walks. Kate Simmons hadn't remarried after her husband passed away. The sisters had often asked her why, hoping to erase the grief. But, with a shake of her head and a fond look in her eyes, Kate always answered by saying, "You can never replace true love once it's gone. I loved your father for thirty years of my life and it was a good life. I can't imagine finding that again." Her parents had shared a love that Jillian hoped to find one day. As strong as she tried to appear, seeing her mother had a way of knocking down her bravado, bringing out the little girl who just needed a hug from her mom.

"My Jillian," her mom softly said, knowing instantly from the phone call that had come hours earlier that her oldest and strongest daughter was hurting, "We'll make it all better," she added, as her daughter flung herself into the open arms that pulled her close into a tight hug.

The tears flowed easily, clouding her vision as her emotions took over. It felt so good to be held by her mom who stroked her hair, whispering words of love and comfort. The story would be told, eventually. For now, she just wanted to savor this moment. The smell of her mother's shampoo, the sweet scent of apples from the pie she had baking in the kitchen for Jillian's homecoming - the smells of home.

Seated at the kitchen table, sunlight streaming through the window that faced the backyard to the west, Jillian sipped the cup of tea her mother had refilled when she had finished telling her story. It had taken over an hour between the tears, questions and moments of silence her mother had let her indulge in. She had a comfortable relationship with her mom that allowed her to easily share her dreams, fears and accomplishments, but had a hard time sharing what she perceived as failures. The events of the past few days certainly could be counted as failures, she had convinced herself. What other explanation was there to account for how she had lost her boyfriend, her job and her home? Even though the wounds were still raw and she was hurting, this re-telling hadn't been that tough with a sympathetic ear to quietly listen and a warm shoulder to cry on.

Her mom seemed to know what she needed to hear at this moment and was able to deliver it succinctly. Plus, having already told Ann, it was becoming an old tale she wanted to move on from.

"Well, Jillian, it certainly is a mess," her mother began after a moment or two of silence, shaking her head as she eyed her daughter from across the table. "It's a mess that's not entirely your fault and the first thing you need to do is realize that. What Kevin did to you was unspeakable, but what's even worse is that your company backed him up for his unforgivable actions. What kind of company practices business like that?" The older woman shook her head in confusion. Having worked in an office in town after the girls were in school, she was all too familiar with office politics.

Her desire to work had been born out of boredom and the desire to stretch her wings, if only a little. She had loved her life; raising her daughters, being an equal partner with her husband while making a loving, warm home for all of them. But the part-time job had been for her something to identify herself with that didn't include titles like Jim's wife or Jillian and Jessica's mom. In her role as receptionist in a doctor's office, she was known as Kate Simmons. That was it. No other titles had been necessary. She'd been her own person without losing the wonderful life she had at home. After Jim's death, she continued to work part-time, turning down promotion offers because she didn't want to make the commitment. When she got tired of working, she would quit and use the retirement funds she and Jim had established. They were going to use the money to travel and see the world together, but the desire to travel wasn't as strong for her as it used to be. It just didn't seem right without Jim.

"I know that mom, but I feel so terrible about everything. I mean, I don't even have an address," Jillian said, that sentence having made her realize that she needed to call the postal office and have her mail forwarded. But where would she have it forwarded? It was all so overwhelming, and as if succumbing to the reality, she dropped her head to the table, with her arms raking through her hair in frustration and confusion. "I don't have a job, I'm the laughing stock of my company, but then again," she paused for a breath, "it's not even my company anymore!" she cried, flailing her arms in the air before dropping her head back down on the table, causing her mother to chuckle at her dramatics.

"Jillian, first you need to calm down. You're not the first person to lose their job. You're also not the first person to be victimized by a bad relationship. What you don't seem to remember is that you are a beautiful, intelligent, skillful person with more potential in one pinkie than in Kevin McBride's entire body! He doesn't deserve another second of your time, so don't give him the luxury of knowing that he's even on your mind."

"You're right, mom and I know that, but..., " her voice trailed off, but Kate didn't seem to notice as she plowed ahead.

"Jillian Simmons, do you remember what your father used to tell you and your sister when you were younger?" she began as her youngest daughter entered the kitchen.

"Hiya, Jillian," Jessica said, greeting her sister with a warm hug. "What's going on? What did dad tell us? What happened? Did you have Kevin have a fight? I never did like him, I didn't trust him, for that matter," she added, helping herself to a slice of the still-warm apple pie. Jessica had always been full of questions, much to her teachers' annoyance. But she had always been a curious child, a characteristic that had apparently stuck with her as she grew older.

"We broke-up, I lost my job and I don't have anywhere to live," Jillian informed her sister. The look on Jessica's face was priceless enough to make Jillian laugh at the absurdity of the statement. Not many people could say they lost all of that in one day. If she had had a pet, she was certain that it would have been run over on that day too, to complete her aura of bad karma.

"Wow," Jessica breathed, becoming silent as she absorbed the seriousness of the situation. Kate continued, "When you girls were younger, your father used to tell you that you could do anything you set your mind to doing. There were no limits on the successes you could achieve. If you experienced a shortcoming or a failure, you had to learn from the experience, pick yourself up and move on."

"I just don't think it's that easy, Mom. I mean, what am I going to do now? Sure, I have enough money saved, that if I live frugally, I won't go hungry for a few months, but then what? I love my job and damn it, I was good at it. I like working and I just... don't know," she added, feeling herself moving out of the stage of depression, hopefully for the last time. It felt good to look on the situation with a touch of anger at something other than herself. Though she knew that it wasn't that easy to walk away - or be forced to walk away - from the things that had been her life for so long. There would undoubtedly be more heartache, tears and unhappiness before she completely healed herself.

Later that evening, when the tears were dried and the story was told, dissected and stored away, they all sat around Kate's large dining room table, enjoying each other's company. When she knew Jillian was coming home, Kate had invited Jessica and her family over for dinner. She thought a good family dinner was exactly what Jillian needed. Good food, pleasant conversation - an evening with family.

Knowing everyone loved her lasagna, Kate made a big pan stuffed with lots of gooey cheese that melted in your mouth. Jessica brought wine and a salad full of delicious fresh veggies from a produce market in town, while Jillian made garlic toast from a loaf of homemade bread.

"Aunt Jilly," Jessica's daughter, Hannah, began while fighting with a long string of cheese from her lasagna. Giving up on capturing the string on her fork, she twirled it around her finger several times before popping it in her mouth. "Will you be here to take me to the park?"

Smiling at the adorable four-year-old with the bouncy curls she'd inherited from her mother, she said, "I think I can manage that, but only if we can go for ice cream afterwards," she added with a wink.

"Yeah!" Hannah and Daniel, Jessica's five-year-old son exclaimed, rushing around the table to hug their aunt. She loved her niece and nephew and enjoyed spoiling them with little treats whenever she could. During most business trips, she made a point to pick up a gift for each of them and send them through the mail, which was a really big deal to them.

"Nobody is going to the park or for ice cream," Jessica warned in a stem voice, finishing her glass of wine and pouring another, "until they clean their plates. Now sit back down and let Aunt Jilly finish her dinner." Everyone knew the stern voice was just for effect.

Jessica's husband, Jack Mason, chimed in, "Maybe if you're really good, Aunt Jilly will tell you your bedtime story tonight."

Vice President of the loan office at the largest bank in the area, Jack had a deep respect and fondness for his sister-in-law. They were good friends and enjoyed one another's company. Like his wife, Jack had never taken to Kevin McBride. The man was too slick and shady for Jack's taste. Plus, he had a roving eye that didn't stop after he began dating and living with Jillian. The two men had tried to get along, for the sake of the Simmons sisters. They even went to a few baseball games together, but Jack didn't trust Kevin and openly shared his feelings with his wife. Since he liked Jillian so much and didn't want to add additional grief to what he saw as a bad relationship, he kept quiet around her.

Jack added, "Jillian you're better off without Kevin and you know it. Furthermore, you're in an interesting position of looking at your life and making a new start. If you don't want to do the same work, don't. If you want to open your own business, do it. If you want to sit back and relax for a few weeks, do it. You're your own boss in charge of your own life, so make the most of it and do what will make you happy. Nobody can tell you what that is, only you can."

"Here here!" Jessica chimed in, raising her refilled wine glass to her sister with a smile. "It's like we're getting the band back together. You haven't lived at home since before college, right Jilly? We've been through a lot since then. It will be nice to have you around to help out with everything."

Kate shot her youngest daughter a warning look that shushed her from continuing whatever she was hinting at, though Jillian caught the undercurrent. Wonder what that's about, she thought, tucking that away for inspection at another time when her brain was clear. She might have been imaging the quick change of temperature between her sister and mother given Kate's pointed look at Jessica that suddenly shut her up.

"Well, I'm definitely glad to be here for mom's lasagna and the company! It sounds like I may have missed something while being a way? How's the wine, Jess, leave any for the rest of us?" Jillian inquired with a smile to take some of the sting out of her question that she hadn't consciously meant to ask out loud, but it seemed like her little sister was getting a little tipsy at family dinner.

"Oh don't worry, I'm sure we can pop open another bottle if you want some," Jessica laughed a little louder than necessary.

Jillian thought that she'd have to keep an eye on her sister and ask her mom if everything was ok with her and Jack. She loved her family, but like most families, theirs had its share of secrets.

CHAPTER 10

When Jillian had lived at home, she loved to walk. That was her favorite exercise because she could do it anywhere and didn't need to invest in a lot of expensive workout equipment, just a good pair of sneakers. After moving out on her own, she continued the nightly regimen. It gave her a chance to unwind after busy and frequently stressful workdays and to enjoy the scenery around her. While on the road, she would head to the hotel's fitness center in whatever city she was visiting and watch the miles go by on a treadmill while watching TV or listening to an audio book. As she grew up and moved away from home, creating a life for herself, she continued with the nightly walks that eventually turned into jogs.

It was during one of these long evening walks that she started to think about the past with a clear head. She had been at her mom's house for the past week and was starting to enjoy the downtime while thinking about getting her life back in order, especially since she didn't spend most of the days crying. She still didn't know what she wanted to do, but had become accustomed to, if not embraced, the idea of being single and alone. It had been a long time since she had the freedom of not being involved with anyone.

Relationships hadn't been her specialty, granted, but she did have fond memories of past boyfriends. Her first real love was her high school boyfriend. They met in grade school, but it wasn't until a ski trip in their sophomore year that they became better acquainted.

Jillian had lost control of her skis, flying down one of the harder trails and crashed into him, who had stopped towards the side of the traffic. He hadn't been upset that she had crashed into him, sending him sprawling into a nearby snow pile, with her landing right on top of him. His first concern, as they untangled from the mess of legs, arms, skis and poles, flung everywhere, was that she wasn't hurt.

"Jillian, are you ok? Did you get break anything?" he had asked, helping her to her feet. He stood a good six inches taller in his ski boots than she did, towering over her.

"No, no, I'm ok," she said, thoroughly embarrassed that she'd plowed into and knocked him down. She didn't make a habit of colliding with the cutest boy in school.

"Are you sure?" he asked, his blue eyes peering deeply into hers, causing her cheeks to flush under his intense gaze. "Here, let's ski down together on the side of the trail where there's less traffic."

Together, they set off down the hill, keeping pace with one another, him making sure she had a mostly clear path to the bottom. She kept an eye on the trail and his green ski coat in front of her. It had been a lovely evening, with temperatures in the lower 40's and a slight breeze off of the mountains. Thanks to the recent snowfall, the slopes were packed, yet powdery as they reached the bottom.

Students from their school and other skiers were milling around, getting on the lifts, knocking into each other and laughing as the fun atmosphere grew. The ski club was one of the most popular at their school, so much so that they always needed more than one bus to transport the kids and their gear for each trip. The more experienced had their own equipment, while the newbies rented what was available. You could also tell who were the experienced with the number of lift tags attached to the zipper on their ski jackets. Jillian's zipper only had one tag, and with the way she was doing, she figured that's all she might ever have.

"How about a hot chocolate? I'm ready for a break. You interested?" he asked with a smile. His cheeks were flushed from the cold, making his blue eyes pop against the striking white background. His brown hair was tousled when he removed his ski cap. Running a hand through it, he clicked his boots out of his skis, ready to go inside.

Her stomach was light and full of butterflies as he turned his smile to her, waiting for her to lead the to the lounge. She was so excited to have had a conversation with him, let alone share hot chocolates in the lodge; it was hard for her to do more than smile and nod. She had a secret crush on Matt for years, since they were in grade school, but never let her feelings known, not wanting to risk ruining their friendship.

They sat in the lounge, facing the ski slopes and watching the other skiers, sipping their hot drinks until their school chaperone announced that the buses would be boarding in fifteen minutes. The bus ride home had been even better than the lodge as they sat huddled together in the seat, arms wrapped around each other as the teenagers kissed tentatively. That had been the start of their relationship that saw them through homecoming dances, proms and eventually senior graduation, when they parted ways, both going to different colleges. Still in love, they promised to keep in touch, but time passed, they both changed. The letters and phone calls came and went with less frequency, until they stopped all together. She hadn't talked to Matt since that summer, but fondly remembered the young love they shared.

She dated sporadically in college, but didn't commit herself to anyone (or anything) except her schoolwork and college jobs. She had ambition and goals that she was determined to reach. The occasional frat party and casual date were enough to keep her socially active, but not too frequent to make her lose sight of why she was in college in the first place. She was there to get a job and learn as much about anything and everything that would prepare her for the working world. With all that in mind, though, she had thoroughly enjoyed college.

Looking back, she didn't regret any of her decisions. She asked her mom a few years after high school if she heard anything about Matt. Kate's only news was that he'd dropped out of college after finishing his first year and was a contractor. Jillian had been disappointed to hear that he hadn't finished college but didn't ask Kate about him again, with her career picking up and not allowing herself much time to dwell on the past.

Her relationship with Kevin began two years after she started working at Williams Consulting. Though she was attracted to him and his charismatic good looks, she hadn't wanted to cross the line of dating the boss. But fate had other ideas for her.

She'd been working late one evening, trying to finish up some paperwork for a business trip she was taking the following morning when Kevin entered his office. He, too, had been burning the midnight oil, and looked beat as he leaned against her office door.

"Jillian, you are the hardest worker in this company, I swear," he said with a sexy, lazy smile that lit up his handsome features.

"Thanks, Kevin," she told her boss with a small smile, making an effort not to notice how broad his shoulders looked in the slightly wrinkled charcoal gray shirt he wore. It was hard not to notice how gorgeous he was. She was definitely attracted to him. Theirs had been a strictly business relationship, though he was a rather affectionate boss, patting her shoulder and finding it necessary to touch her, though lightly, when he talked to her. She knew she was imagining things when she thought his affection was more than business. That was just the way he was, she reasoned. And in the wake of the Hollywood sex scandals, she should have been offended, but she wasn't.

"How about joining me for a drink?" he asked, with an electric smile showing his perfect white teeth. "Oh, I'd love to, but I still have some things to get done before my trip tomorrow. Remember, I'm going to meet with Johnson Brothers for their pitch. I want to make a good impression on them and need to be fluent about their business goals," she said, referencing the major client she was wooing for the company.

"You're going to be incredible, as you always are," he said softly, closing the office door behind him and advancing toward her. "Tell me something, Jillian. Why is it that you and I have never gone out on a date?" he asked, standing right in front of her now.

Jillian stood up, surprised at the closeness of Kevin's body to her own. She shivered slightly as he rubbed his strong hands up and down her bare arms, the heat from his fingers surging through her body. Moaning slightly at the touch and feel of him so close, so intimate, to her, she cleared her throat.

"Because I work for you," she answered, her voice husky, barely above a whisper.

"So, what you're saying," he started to say, reaching around and releasing her long, auburn hair from the confines of the clip she had fastened at the base of her neck. Her hair fell softly around her shoulders in a mass of waves. He concentrated on gently running his hands through the tresses, working the hair this way and that, gently pulling on the strands. "Is that if you didn't work for me, there wouldn't be a problem, hmm? Well, look at that," he said with a glance at his watch, "it's after 8:00, well past normal business hours."

He leaned in and started kissing her neck, his breath hot on her cool skin, causing her to tremble slightly at the contact. Unable to control herself, she ran her hands through his hair, throwing her head back, giving him access to her collarbone, where he was feathering her skin with light kisses. After several moments of attending to her neck and ear lobes, he kissed his way to her full, red lips where she hungrily greeted him in a passionate kiss that left them both breathless and a little dizzy

From that moment on, they'd been an item. Though she knew how it had happened, she still couldn't believe she was dating her boss. That wasn't her style. The age difference between them was nominal, but the fact that she worked for him was hard for her to overcome at times. It was just awkward in the office, but Kevin admonished her for thinking like that.

Sure, she had been attracted to Kevin and, though she hated to admit it now, she 'd been in love with him. She just felt like such a fool! It wasn't like her to fall in love so easily and lose her vision and sense of self. He had romanced her, splurged on lavish gifts and weekends away, that she started to lose sight of everything else. She'd been so wrapped up in what Kevin wanted to do, what made Kevin happy, that she forgot about herself along the way. Granted, she lived a fabulous life and never went without anything she wanted, but part of that was because her needs were simple. Extravagant wealth and expensive trinkets didn't impress her. She much preferred a picnic lunch to a cocktail party with caviar and champagne.

It took her a while to realize that her job performance had started to slip a notch or two, nothing noticeable by others. But, being the perfectionist she was, she hadn't been giving her clients all of her time and attention.

Of course, it was easier for her to blame Kevin for the things that had recently gone wrong in her life, but she could also look at it as a learning experience.

Don't forget your sense of self and give up what you want just to make someone else happy. It's not worth the price you pay. She was just lucky that her family was so supportive and understanding. They were giving her the time and space she needed to heal and move on with her life. Always a resilient person, Jillian was never one to wallow in self-pity for long. It was time to get on with her life and focus on the future, not worry about the past. But, as is the case with some things that are easier said than done, it's not always that easy to let go, though you know it's for the best.

But, she was getting bored. It had only been a week and already she could feel the nothingness settling in. For the first few days, it just seemed like she was on vacation; an extended vacation, of course. But, nonetheless, it didn't really feel like she was jobless, just out of the office for a few days.

She'd been filling her days with long talks with her mother and her sister, jogs around the neighborhood and town that had been so familiar once upon a time and were still native to her, even now. But, that didn't seem like enough to fill the long, empty days. She missed the daily conversations in the office with her friends and associates, the long, sometimes boring conference calls with clients. They were only boring and stressful when she hadn't been given the correct information to satisfy the demands of her sometimes needy clients. Those situations were out of her control but she missed the energy and travel of her job.

She waited a few days before responding to the texts from some of her former work friends, but those wouldn't last long, she knew. She was out of the loop on happenings in the office. Everyone always says they'll stay in touch, but when you don't get the new punch lines or references, it's time to let go and move on. She'd been texting Ann, though, who always kept her spirits up.

Ann knew everything anyway, so texting her was easy. She somehow managed to make Jillian chuckle at some of the memes she sent her. It was funny how they could communicate simply through memes that fit the situation or made the other one laugh out loud. But now, she didn't even want to talk to Ann, not knowing what to say that she hadn't already said.

She wasn't ready to look at her LinkedIn profile. She thought saying she was downsized sounded better than fired. The phrasing didn't seem as hopeless as saying she got fired. She figured she'd update LinkedIn and social media when she had something to say.

CHAPTER 11

Arriving early to the jobsite, Matt surveyed the property and ran the plans through his head once again. The house they were working on was basically a split-level in the front, with nothing obstructing the back of the house. Adding a new room would be a fairly simple process, since there weren't any foundation issues to contend with - they were building onto the existing three-car garage under the house. It was going to be a pretty straightforward project. He'd known the homeowners for years and was looking forward to the project.

Knowing it would be a busy day, he'd brought his softball clothes and equipment with him and would go straight to the field from work, after stopping for a quick dinner on the way. It would be another long day, but he was used to that.

His crew started arriving a few minutes later. It was almost 7:00 a.m. and they had a full day ahead of them. He liked starting the day early, especially in the summer. Once they hit noon, the sun was high in the sky overhead, shining down on them.

Around noon, as his crew was breaking for lunch in the shade of an old oak tree on the property, he took a few minutes to review the plans for the rest of the day with his project manager and then left.

Across town, he had another jobsite to visit. His second crew was doing a roof, and he wanted to check their progress. A couple days of rain last week had caused him to adjust his schedule, but you just couldn't plan the weather.

Mentally going through his calendar, he tried to figure out the jobs he had lined up for the next several months. They were doing a commercial roof on the local fire department's social hall. That should last about a week if he diverted his larger crew to that project. Then his smaller crew could start the demo on a kitchen he was remodeling across town. He had a new three-car garage planned for the end of the month before both of his crews were scheduled to refurbish an old barn one of his wealthier clients wanted to remodel as a photography studio. That was a big job, but with both crews tackling it all day, they should be able to finish it in a week, maybe a week and a half depending on the weather.

As any contractor tries to do, he lined up his outdoor projects when the weather was the nicest and reserved indoor work for the months when it was too cold to work outside. Paint doesn't dry in winter any more than it does in the heavy humidity in mid-summer. The kitchen remodel was pushed up by a few months at his client's insistence. As a small business owner, he had to do some negotiating and make some concessions to keep his reputation as a hard-working, honest contractor positive.

When he first started his business years ago, he invested in cases of the personalized merchandise like pencils, calendars, magnets and the like with his company's name on it. That marketing plan worked and helped him establish his business. Since then, it's been word of mouth, his reputation and work that draw in the work. He usually spends a few days a week out making sales calls as his phone and home answering machine fill with call from prospective clients. He realized a long time ago that having a bunch of messages to return was a good problem to have.

It still gave him a sense of pride when he drove his truck with the name of his construction company on the side. At this point, he had a small fleet of trucks, work vans, trailers, work equipment and supplies at a small garage he used to rent across town. Once his business took off and started showing profit and durability, he bought the property and expanded the garage to house more equipment as his calendar filled with jobs outside of their small town. He'd become a reputable name in the industry and became involved in local politics - a way to give back to the community that supported him as an up and coming businessman.

CHAPTER 12

Unable to resist the urge any longer, she picked up the phone and dialed the number. She didn't even have to look it up. Maybe it wasn't a good idea, but she simply couldn't wait another minute. It was a number she'd memorized - she had called it enough times over the past few years. In fact, she didn't even have to look at the numbers on the phone while she dialed. Her fingers automatically went to the next number, executing a well-rehearsed routine. Sucking in her breath as the phone began to ring, she questioned the wisdom of her call. She wasn't committing a crime. It's a free country; she's allowed to call and ask a few questions. It's not like she's harassing anyone – or him.

Certainly, she had a right to know why. Well, obviously she knew why, but it just didn't make any sense and she wasn't satisfied with the information – or lack thereof - she had been given. He was going to have to give her a better answer than that.

"Good afternoon, Williams Consulting. How may I direct your call?" the receptionist chirped her greeting. Jillian didn't know her well and hoped that she didn't recognize her voice. The last thing she needed was for her phone call to him to be the latest nugget of office gossip. She was sure she'd been discussed daily since her departure. That's how office gossip worked. Information was passed on as soon as it was learned. Whether it was true or not, embellished or accurate, the news spread through the office at the speed of light. She'd been guilty of gossiping too. Sometimes the news was too good to not pass on.

She waited impatiently after giving the receptionist the extension number and felt silly for having slightly disguised her voice. Laughing at herself, she reflected that she wasn't a secret agent or a spy whose life depended on the secrecy of nobody knowing her identity. She had definitely watched too many movies and read too many books. "Bond, James Bond," she laughed at herself as she did her best 007.

"Human Relations, this is John," the caller identified himself.

"Hi, John, this is Jillian. How are you?" she inquired, sounding more upbeat than she actually felt at the moment. Her stomach was in knots and her voice had a slight quiver when she spoke. But, she needed to know.

"Jillian, this is a surprise. How are you doing? Where are you?" John asked anxiously.

"I'm doing alright, John, thanks for asking. I won't take up much of your time," she said as he indicated that he always had time for her. "I was calling," she started, and then paused to clear her throat. "I was calling to talk about the way I was dismissed from Williams Consulting. I'm not at all happy with the events that took place," she began, gaining confidence as she continued. "I feel that I was poorly treated and that possible legal action could be taken on my part since I was released for something that happened in my personal life, not my professional life."

"Well, Jillian, I'm afraid that's just not true. You were released because of the complaints we received from some of your clients," he said, sounding suddenly all business-like, not friendly, as he had been during the beginning of the conversation.

"Oh, come on, John," she said, irritated that he would continue to tell her that. "Which clients complained about me and what were their complaints? Why didn't my manager bring them to my attention when the complaints were lodged? Wouldn't that have been the proper procedure?"

"The complaints had been communicated a few days before you... ah... your release. So, there wasn't time to have a formal review with you, which would have been the proper procedure," he explained, hating his job at that moment more than he ever had. "I'm sorry, but there's really nothing you can do about it, Jillian," he added in a softer tone.

"I just don't think it's fair," she said in a smaller voice, losing most of her bravado as she realized that he was right. They had certainly covered their tracks well.

"Jillian, where are you? Have you found another job? Is there anything I can do to help?"

"I'm visiting my mom. I needed to get away and out of town so that I could clear my head and think about what I want to do. It's still so hard to believe. I mean, John, I put a lot of time and effort into my job and then I get kicked out the door because of Kevin. Don't try to deny it, we both know that's the reason I was fired. You don't have to admit it. I know you're in an awkward position as it is, and that they made up the story of client complaints. You know what, I don't even care anymore. I just want to sever all ties with Williams Consulting and move on with my life," she finished.

"Well, if you need a reference, you know you can count on me. Personally, I think they made a big mistake in letting you go. It's going to be our loss in the long run. What's your mom's address? I have some paperwork to send to you," John said, the two of them returning to talking like the friends they were.

She ended the call with a sad sigh. She wasn't angry with John. It wasn't his fault. He was just the messenger; he was only doing his job. She had given him her mom's address. She wasn't sure how long she was going to be there, but she didn't want any of her mail going to Kevin's house. In fact, she needed to get to the post office and have her mail forwarded. She still hadn't gotten around to that. When she had left town, she didn't know what to do about her mail, but figured her mom's address could be her temporary address.

Before settling in to take a nap since she didn't know what else to do, she heard her phone ping. Groaning, she grabbed the phone and gave it a cautious glance. Was John texting her? Or maybe Kevin had heard that she called and he was texting her. She was tempted to not look, and then saw that it was Ryan.

"Ugh, I definitely can't take this," she murmured out loud as she powered down her phone and crawled further under the blankets. Her life had been turned completely upside down in a matter of hours, no, minutes, and she didn't know what to do. When in doubt, napping and crying are a good combination, she thought, closing her eyes to the sun shining in the window.

CHAPTER 13

Wandering around her mother's house aimlessly had become her daily routine when Jillian wasn't napping or crying. It wasn't that she wanted to be depressed, but there just didn't seem to be an alternative to the emptiness and loneliness that had invaded her life. She tried not to cry in front of her mother anymore; she didn't want her to worry about her more than she already was.

She'd always been a happy, optimistic person, but the blows she'd recently been dealt seemed to change her outlook and the way she interacted with the world. It wasn't just that she lost her job or her boyfriend, or even her home, which wasn't really her home after all. The feelings she had ran deeper than that. It was more a question of her self-worth.

Right now, it was at an all-time low, a feeling she had never experienced - with the exception, perhaps, of her father's death. That was a time in her life, in all of their lives, when it didn't seem as though the sun would ever shine again.

What was there to laugh about anymore? Why bother pretending that everything was all right and that tomorrow would be better than today, when everyone knew that their lives had changed dramatically? Her emotions had been on an emotional rollercoaster.

The days seemed longer than they really were, especially when she saw the productive life her mother had made for herself. Kate was up before dawn on the days she worked, enjoying a cup of coffee and a muffin while reading the paper. Then she went off to work, where she had a purpose, and came home to her house where Jillian had set up her own pity party. That's how she thought her mother saw her these days. Try as she might, she just couldn't seem to get on with her life and she knew her mother's patience was being strained as a result. Certainly, she didn't question her mother's love or support. She just knew that she was a disappointment, and that was the one thing she couldn't take. Even while growing up, learning about the world and the woman she would someday become, she never wanted to disappoint her parents. Seeing the look of sadness in her mother's eyes was enough to make Jillian want to get up each day and try to go on with her life. Even Jessica had started to question what she did with herself all day. What would her sister say if she knew that Jillian, her older, seemingly wiser sister, wandered the house aimlessly all day in her pajamas, not even bothering to shower or brush her hair some days. For someone who had been on the go constantly the past few years, she sure embraced wallowing in the downtime.

Getting on with her life wasn't going to happen if she didn't make it happen. The call with John had made her realize that nobody in the office really missed her, since she was out of the office so much of the time anyway for travel. Sure, they had asked about her, but did they really walk by her office and wonder what she was doing or how she was? Maybe at first for a couple of days after her dismissal, people talked and wondered, but what about now? Had they already begun to overlook her absence and move on with their own lives, forgetting about her? She suspected that she'd become someone who used to work there at one time, but didn't anymore. As her former co-workers moved on and assumed new positions with new companies, would they even remember working with Jillian Simmons? Had she made a lasting impression with anyone there? She wondered these things but vowed not to obsess over it. She'd start thinking about her future tomorrow.

And, what was going on between her mother and sister? She hadn't forgotten about the sudden tension between them during family dinner. Had something happened that she didn't know about?

CHAPTER 14

Racing from the porch to grab the ringing telephone, Jillian reached it on the third ring, "Hello?" she asked, slightly breathless from the race to the phone.

"Hey, it's Jess. What're ya doing? You sound like you're out of breath."

"I was sitting out on the porch reading and had to run into the kitchen to get the phone. Mom went to a dinner with friends from work tonight, so I was just hanging out. What's up?"

"Mom's always going somewhere and you've had enough downtime. Jack has a softball game tonight and the kids and I are planning on going. I called to see if you wanted to tag along. You'll probably run into some old friends at the field, and it'll do you good to get out of the house," the younger sister added the last as a mild lecture to the older sister.

It was true, she knew - she'd been staying close to home the past few days. She arrived a few weeks ago and hadn't left the house longer than a jog or a quick trip to the store. It wasn't that she was avoiding seeing people she knew, she was just enjoying the comforts of sleeping in and doing nothing all day; at least that's what she told herself. She still hadn't solved the problem of what to do for work. She had actually called an attorney and discussed the possibility of suing Williams Consulting. But the lawyer had advised against it, as it would be too hard to prove the allegations, added to the fact that she had been in a long-term personal relationship with her boss. John had been correct, but she felt mildly better that she had at least contacted an attorney.

"I don't know, Jess," she protested.

"Well, we'll be there in half an hour, so get yourself ready!" Jessica ordered before hanging up the phone.

With a small smile, Jillian replaced the phone in its hook. Jess had a way of bullying her into doing what she wanted. She was the kind of person who would push and push until you did whatever it was that she wanted, just to shut her up. Jillian loved her for it and didn't want her to change one bit. It was part of her charm and a great personality trait.

The sisters were alike in a lot of ways, but also different. Jillian was tall with long auburn hair, brown eyes and a firm, athletic body. She liked working out and worked hard to keep her body in shape. Indulgences like cheesecake and burgers almost instantly made a beeline for her hips, whereas Jessica could eat anything in sight and not gain an ounce, much to Jillian's envy. She recently had her blonde hair cut into a lob that looked effortlessly chic.

The differences didn't end with their physical appearance. Jillian was the career woman. She'd gone to college immediately after high school, working and taking extra classes to get as complete an education as possible. She dated a few people, nobody too serious, until Kevin. Their relationship was the longest she'd had since high school.

Jessica, on the other hand, hadn't gone on to college after high school. She enrolled in the teller-training program at First Bank and Trust. Naturally chatty and personable, she loved working as a bank teller and was liked by her co-workers. She was able to catch up with her customers, most of whom had known her all her life. Her life had taken a dramatic change, however, when Jack Mason was hired to lead the loan department. She'd instantly fallen in love with the black-haired, blue-eyed six-foot-tall Vice President. The feeling had been mutual and they were married six months later. Now, a few years and two kids later, they seemed just as much in love as they were when they first met. Jessica quit her job when Daniel had been born, devoting her time to being a full-time mom. Jillian hadn't had much time to really talk to Jessica and seeing her indulge in extra wine gave her pause. She made a mental reminder to check on her little sister when they had time alone, just to make sure she was ok.

Jillian ran upstairs to freshen up before Jessica and her family arrived. With a glance in the mirror, she was glad to see that her hours sitting in the sun in the backyard had added a healthy glow to her skin, with the weather getting warmer every day. She always tanned easily and without much effort, much to her fair-skinned sister's annoyance. Jessica burned while sitting in the shade. After a quick spray of dry shampoo, she brushed out her hair and let it fall in natural waves that framed her face. She added a touch of mascara and lip-gloss, dabbed a bit of perfume on her wrists and behind her ears, then went to find something to wear. Since it was a softball game, casual attire of shorts and sandals was the norm. She remembered hanging out at the games with her group of friends in high school. Of course, she had been there to cheer on Matt. After the games, their gang would head to town for pizza to celebrate the team's victory or cheer them up if they happened to lose, which wasn't often. With a wistful smile, she closed her eyes and remembered the fun they used to have. But, she thought, as much fun as it had been, she wouldn't want to go back to high school or her teenage years for anything in the world! Unless she could take what she knew today with her, that is.

Several minutes later, she settled on a pair of soft, slightly faded denim shorts that stopped several inches above her knees, exposing her tanned, toned thighs and a white tank top that she tucked into the waistband of her shorts. She was glad she had grabbed some of her summer clothes from the storage facility. The temperature had been getting warm since she arrived, and she'd been living in shorts and tank tops around the house. Slipping her feet into a pair of black sandals, she added gold hoop earrings as a car horn sounded outside. After writing a quick note for her mom, she grabbed a set of house keys and headed out the front door.

Until she was walking around the ballpark with Jessica and the kids, she hadn't realized how excited she was to be there. Not just at the game, but back at home, even if only for a visit. It felt good to be outside, enjoying the fun of summer with family and friends she'd known for a lifetime. Seeing several people she knew, she chatted easily, taking in the sights and sounds of the ballpark. The slow pace and relaxed atmosphere rejuvenated her spirit, making her start to realize everything she'd been missing out on while living life on the "fast track." Her life had revolved around meetings, conference calls, frequent flyer miles, working lunches and so on. She couldn't believe how busy her life had been and how she managed to cram so much into one day. There wasn't much time left to do the things she wanted to do. Thanks to the recent change of events, her life was slower and less hectic. That wasn't necessarily a bad thing either. But, she didn't think she could sit idle forever. Her bank account was still healthy, but it wasn't an endless supply of money.

They chose seats off of the first base line on the bleachers where half of the town was already seated, waiting for the first pitch. Jillian had treated for snow cones, and Hannah and Daniel were busy slurping up the sugary blue ice, trying to catch it before it melted. Jilliaj and Jessica were sharing an order of nachos with cheese and jalapeno peppers and two large cokes. Laughing, she tried to scoop up a nacho with cheese, while avoiding the jalapenos that Jessica loved.

"Thanks, Jessie, this is just what I needed. You know, I haven't seen this many people from high school since I graduated."

"Oh, I just knew you'd have a good time tonight!" Jessica replied. "You just needed to get out of the house and 'out among the people,' as dad used to say."

"Or, 'get the stink blown off me,' as Gram would have said?" Jillian quipped about the grin Jessica was trying unsuccessfully to hide. Before Jessica was forced to answer, the game began.

"Now batting, first baseman, Jack Mason," the announcer called out as Jack approached the plate, kicking around the dirt at home plate. He was the leadoff hitter for the team and always a good player.

"Yeah, Daddy!" Hannah and Daniel jumped up and cheered in unison, dripping their blue snow cone on the ground, just missing Jillian's leg. "Hit a homerun!"

Jack hit a single and was forced to slide into first base as the first basemen for the visiting team nearly tagged him out. Dirty and full of dust, he got up and waved to his kids who were jumping up and down jubilantly, smiling blue, sticky smiles while the crowd cheered along.

"Yeah, Daddy!" they cheered again, with Jessica and Jillian joining in the fun. If the weather earlier in the day was any indication, the evening was going to be just as beautiful, even when the sun went down. The ballpark was shared by the school district as well as the community sports teams. It was fairly new, having only been built four years ago. It was a modern facility with dugouts for each team, a concession stand, restrooms, and bleacher seating that could easily accommodate the fans from both teams. There was even a small playground beyond the outfield where kids could entertain themselves. A fund-drive, including donations from local businesses and corporate sponsors, made the park possible. The press box, located in the stands directly behind and slightly elevated above home plate, was always a hub of activity. Local reporters watched the game from there while the play-by-play announcers called the game.

"Now batting, Matt Parker," called the announcer from the press box as number thirteen stepped into the batter's box.

Jillian sucked in her breath as number thirteen stepped into the batter's box. "Jessica," she hissed, "why didn't you tell me Matt was on Jack's team?!"

"Oh," Jessica commented innocently, "it must have slipped my mind." Feeling her sister's eyes on her, she glanced at her with a grin and a wink, "I thought you needed a good distraction, and what could be a better distraction than Matt Parker, most eligible bachelor in a three-county area, not to mention the hottest contractor around. Maybe he'll model his tool belt for you later, sis!" Jessica added with a laugh and lecherous wiggle of her eyebrows.

The part about Matt being hot was definitely true. She couldn't deny that Matt still looked as handsome as he had in high school, but the batter's helmet he wore made it hard to tell for sure. The light brown hair that peeked out of the back of the helmet still curled at the nape of his neck. She recalled running her hands through the thick tresses while making out in the old Mustang he drove in high school. They sure did have a good time, but were too young and afraid to do much more than make out. Theirs was a young romance full of lust and naivety, laced with ample energy and youth. When she thought of high school, she couldn't help but think of Matt Parker.

But she wasn't in high school anymore; she was a grown woman, though she did feel a little giddy as she watched him run around the bases. He hit a homerun, sending Jack to home plate too. He easily jogged around the bases, a lazy grin on his face as if he was used to hitting home runs. Somehow, he still had an effect on her.

The fans were all on their feet, shouting and cheering for the home team who was winning the game, thanks to the baseball skills that Matt apparently hadn't lost after high school. He had been up to bat four times and managed to hit a homerun, a single before stealing second, and a double. His work in the field allowed the home team to keep their three-run lead. She continued to study him throughout the game, admiring the man he had become.

Wonder what he's still doing in town, she thought. Jessica said something about him still being a bachelor. When she turned to ask her sister, she noticed that she was involved in a conversation with another young mother sitting next to her. She returned to her daydreaming. Well, if he was on the softball team, she reasoned, he must still live and work in town.

It was amazing that the questions and thoughts about Matt were flooding her mind when she hadn't thought about him in years. They were an item in high school, but that was a long time ago, though the memories were strong.

Looking at the field where he stood in the outfield, she could tell that he'd grown into an extremely handsome man. He was still tall, having topped out at over six feet she guessed. The brown hair was the same - it looked as thick and wavy as it had always been. With a slight shudder, she remembered his eyes and the depth of color she'd seen there. They were deep blue, like the sea, and just as mesmerizing as the rise and fall of the tide. She could look into his eyes for hours, lost. He had a way of grinning that used to make her go weak in the knees, while her heart practically melted into a puddle. What a charmer he had been, she thought, a dopey smile fixed on her face.

"Jillian," Jessica said impatiently, "Are you deaf? I must have just said your name four or five times."

"Oh sorry," she said, clearing the huskiness from her throat as the daydream vanished, "I was thinking. Um, about work and everything," she trailed off, hoping Jessica wouldn't suspect what she'd really been thinking about. She'd be embarrassed if her sister found out she had been having lustful daydreams about her old high school boyfriend.

"I'm taking Hannah to the restroom, could you keep an eye on Daniel for me?"

"Oh, sure, no problem," Jillian replied, relieved. She smiled at Daniel, who had scooted a little closer to her so that their legs were now touching. "We'll be just fine, won't we Danny boy?" she asked, tickling him in the ribs. Daniel squealed in delight as they watched Jessica and Hannah head off towards the restrooms on the other side of the concession stand.

"Aunt Jillian," the little boy began, looking shyly up at his aunt, "You're not going away again, are you?"

With a smile at his innocent question that was more complicated than if he'd asked her to explain the theory of relativity, she hugged him and said, "Not tomorrow, Danny, but I might have to go back home and back to work. But, don't you worry about that."

"I miss you when you're not here," the boy said, hugging his aunt very tightly, his little hands clenching her in a firm grasp.

A strange feeling came over her as she kissed him lightly on his head. She almost felt a little empty and hollow inside. Her niece and nephew were very important parts of her life and she did her best to stay in touch with them. It again reminded her that she'd chosen a different path in life than her sister. Daniel jumped up again as the home team scored another run, and the feeling and thoughts passed as she joined in the cheering.

CHAPTER 15

After the game, the kids raced down the stands and onto the field where they greeted their father with hugs and shouts of congratulations for the team's win. Though hot and sweaty, Jack had scooped both of them up and twirled them around while their giggles rang out through the cheers and conversation.

Jessica and Jillian followed at a slower pace. Jillian wasn't sure if she was ready to see Matt and was just about to tell Jessica that she'd meet them at the car when she saw him. He was leaning with one hip against the chain link fence that surrounded the park, talking with of the other's team players, his eyes dazzling in the early evening sunlight. His gaze met hers and instant recognition sparked in his eyes, a slow smile spreading across his tanned face. My goodness, she thought, he hadn't changed one bit.

He was still drop-dead gorgeous; with the sexiest smile she had ever seen. The look he gave her was friendly and surprised at the same time, which led her to believe that he hadn't known she was in town.

Returning his smile with a broad grin of her own, Jillian laughed and said, "Hi, Matt," feeling like a schoolgirl again, as she slowly approached him.

Excusing himself from his conversation, Matt continued to look at her with a smile as he strolled over to her, "Well, well. Nice to see you, Jillian Simmons. How long has it been?" His voice was husky and sexy, just like she remembered.

She suddenly found herself nervous, talking with Matt again after all of those years. Memories of their past and relationship flooded her mind as images dart in and out. Now standing directly in front of him, she's more anxious than ever, which doesn't make sense. She's a grown woman, a mature woman, a professional businesswoman, not a high school girl with a crush again. Nervousness didn't make sense. Of course, part of the reason that she was nervous could be attributed to the sexy smile that he focused in her direction. Or, it could be his drop-dead gorgeous appearance that hadn't changed at all since last time she saw him. Even dirty and sweaty from the softball game he just played, he still looked incredible.

"I don't think I've seen you since the summer we graduated from high school. I didn't go back to any of the class reunions, did you?" she asked, finding herself annoyingly nervous. When she was nervous, she had a tendency to talk a lot, unsure what else to do to calm down. Williams Consulting and Kevin McBride were far from her thoughts now. She felt transported back to when she was a high school senior, flirting with the hottest guy in school after their game.

"Well, let's see," he started, absently rubbing his chin as he thought about his answer, "I was out of town for the first one and didn't have time to worry about a class reunion. But I want to know why you aren't giving an old friend a hug, Jillian?" he asked with his arms outstretched towards her.

Taking a few short steps, she walked closer to him as he hugged her in a warm embrace, gently patting her on the back as she involuntary sighed deeply as he enveloped her in a big hug. He smelled of sweat, shampoo and freshly mowed grass, a good combination. She could feel the strong muscles in his back and shoulders, as his arms held her tightly. She wondered if he worked out in a gym or if the firm physique came from hard, manual labor. Didn't Jessica say that Matt was a contractor? If that was the case, he definitely earned the muscles and deep, golden tan from long hard days working outside. Trying not to inhale too deeply, she took in his scent. The entire intoxicating combination was completely, totally and utterly male. She found herself go slightly weak in the knees, her stomach light and airy.

"Ah, excuse me, Jillian and Matt, Jack and I are going to take the kids home," Jessica said with a grin as she approached her sister. "I don't want to interrupt your reunion, so maybe Matt can give you a ride back to mom's house."

"No, no, that's ok," Jillian said, suddenly anxious to remove herself from the possibility of another physical exchange with Matt Parker. The feelings inside were making her nervous and she wasn't quite ready to focus on them too intently.

"Well, now that you mention it," Matt started, "I was about to ask Jillian to split a celebratory pizza with me in town so we can catch-up."

"Great! Well, it's settled then!" Jessica said, walking

towards her family who was already ahead of her towards their car in the parking lot. "I'll talk to you tomorrow, Jilly. Bye!" She didn't want to give her sister a chance to decline Matt's invitation.

"Ok then, I need to take a shower and change before we go anywhere near a restaurant, so we'll have to swing by my house for a few minutes. Is pizza ok with you?

"Is the pizza place still there?" she asked, temporarily giving in to the moment, though every warning bell and buzzer in her body were telling her to turn around and just walk away. Matt Parker had a way of making her lose her senses.

"Matt, I'm sure you're tired. Don't feel obligated to take me to dinner. I can always catch up with Jessica and Jack. I don't want to interrupt your evening."

"It's not an obligation. I don't know about you, but I'm pretty hungry after working up an appetite on the field. Let's go."

CHAPTER 16

While Matt was in the shower, Jillian had a chance to walk around his house and get to know him again. It was always telling to see how someone lived and what their house was like. It's not like she was snooping or anything, she told herself. Matt had told her to make herself comfortable and at home, so she was. It was still such an odd feeling to think that ten years after high school and breaking-up, that she was walking around Matt Parker's house while he was getting ready to take her to dinner. Well, not dinner exactly, but a post-game pizza. Unbelievable! A few weeks ago, she'd lost her job, found out that her boyfriend was cheating on her with a co-worker and now, here she was, going out with her high school boyfriend. If you'd have told her that, she'd have laughed out loud. But, it was just dinner. Don't read more into the evening than was actually there, she told herself. They were just two old friends catching up over pizza. Not exactly a romantic evening between lovers. Then again, Matt wasn't the kind of guy who needed a lot of luxury in his life. He had never been one to try and impress someone with money. She recalled that he liked the simpler things in life, like a good book, going for long walks, pizza and beer, hanging out with family and friends. He didn't require seven courses at every meal and felt more comfortable in Levi's and a flannel shirt than a suit. Kind of how she felt, though dressing up was certainly required for her job. Which wasn't her job anymore, she reminded herself. Actually, the thought of not having to get up at 5:30 a.m., showering, eating breakfast and racing out the door before 7:00 was kind of nice. She wouldn't have to worry about going to bed early so that she could get enough sleep to make it through the long days. Maybe this wasn't going to be so bad for a little while, she thought. Eventually, she'd have to get another job, but she wasn't going to worry about that tonight. She heard the shower stop and continued surveying his home.

Her eyes settled on the mantle of the fireplace at one end of the room where she noticed several snapshots arranged in silver frames of various sizes. There were several of a little girl she guessed to be around five or six years old, about the same age as her nephew, Daniel. She wondered who she was. She certainly was cute, with her light brown hair, small face and bright blue eyes that looked a lot like Matt's. Maybe she was his sister's daughter, she reasoned, when she saw a picture of him and a woman who had to be his sister, Susan. She'd graduated from high school two years after they did. There were other photos - his parents at Christmas, the little girl riding a tricycle in the park, and a group of guys at a ballpark. All in all, if she could make any guesses about his life from these pictures, she would have to say that he was quite happy and successful.

Looking around her, she was impressed with Matt's house. He said that he'd done all of the remodeling work himself when he had the time in between jobs. But, his company and customers had been keeping him so busy for so long, that the house was actually getting remodeled in stages. For instance, he'd re-done the living room, adding a long, wide stone hearth and beautiful wood mantle. There were tall windows on either side with deep wooden window seats beneath each window. The windows looked onto the deck he'd added on the back of the house and the yard beyond. Without seeing all of the area, she liked what she saw. There were flowering trees, white and pink dogwoods mixed with azaleas, hydrangeas and some green shrubs creating a gorgeous palette of bright, lush colors against the dense, dark green of the grass and forest in the background. She was a little surprised to see the small beach area at the lake.

"Ready?" he asked, coming down the stairs. He had changed into jeans and a white polo shirt with his company's name stitched neatly over the left side. His hair was still slightly damp and curling at the nape of his neck. As he walked to the door she was standing in front of, she could smell his aftershave. She recognized the scent as Polo, an old favorite of his and one that she'd bought him for Christmas many years ago.

"Sure," she replied, "I was just admiring your beautiful yard. It's so inviting. Makes you just want to sit on the deck and watch the trees bloom," she added.

She could feel his eyes on her and felt herself blush under his intense scrutiny. Twirling around her, she caught his eye and smiled shyly. "Your living room is very lovely. I must say, I'm quite impressed with your skills as a contractor if you did all of this yourself."

"Well," he started, pushing his hands deep into his front pockets, "it was a lot of planning, time and work. But, it was worth it. Come on, let's go so we can get a table quickly."

CHAPTER 17

Sitting in a booth at the pizza shop across from Matt, she wondered how they had gotten to this point. How quickly things can change! Earlier this morning, she hadn't even thought of Matt in years. Now she was in a booth across from him in their old high school hangout, the Pizza Parlor. It seemed as though Friday nights were still the busiest for the small shop in the heart of the downtown.

It was a busy area, with most of the shops and restaurants in town making up the downtown district. The place hadn't changed a bit since the last time she was there. She glanced around, soaking up the atmosphere that reminded her of high school. Scattered throughout the restaurant were fifteen or so tables, most of which were already filled with the evening dinner crowd.

Booths lined the wall of the shop against the windows that faced out onto the main street. Apparently, it was still a popular eatery for the high school crowd as well, since most of the restaurant was full of boisterous, loud conversations from the teenagers. Music blared from the old jukebox in the corner, and several kids played pool and threw darts as they waited for their food to be ready.

Through the open window to the kitchen, they could see pizza dough being tossed high into the air and expertly caught by the chef who was preparing the hot, delicious, cheesy pizzas. There seemed to be a steady stream of traffic coming in and out of the restaurant as they patiently waited for their order to be taken. Customers were coming in to pick-up their take-out orders as delivery drivers loaded their arms and headed out the door again while the orders were still piping hot.

Settling on a large pizza with pepperoni, mushrooms and extra cheese with a house salad, they ordered drinks. He opted for a draft beer as she requested a glass of red wine as they eased into a comfortable conversation, catching up on the last decade of their lives.

"I can't believe it's been years since I saw you," he murmured.

"I know what you mean. I was just thinking the same thing. I can't believe that we haven't seen each other since Johnny Perry's end of summer party at the lake. That was a night to remember," she added with a smile as they both recalled the legendary party. "What have you been doing for the last ten or so years?"

"Well, after high school, I started at the community college, finished my first year, then decided the academic world and I weren't meant to be, so I dropped out. It made my parents upset and worried that I was going to be a bum, but I had other plans. I started working with a construction crew and learned as much as I could. I liked the work and the feeling of molding something with my hands. I own my own business and I like being my own boss. I have a crew of ten guys that work for me.'

"Wow, Matt," Jillian said in amazement, "you've really done well for yourself. You should proud of all of your accomplishments."

"It's a good feeling at the end of the day. Tell me what you've been doing. I run into your mom and sister occasionally, and Jack during softball season," he smiled.

"Well, I earned my degree in business management and finished in three and a half years. I was anxious to get out into the real world and get my feet wet. I tried a couple of different jobs along the way, until I found my niche as an account executive." Suddenly remembering recent events that brought her back home, she turned silent.

"That's it, now I'm home visiting my family," she ended lamely. She cringed, thinking she was talking too much.

Matt was confused by the sudden change in Jillian. One minute, she was enthusiastic about her life, and then she abruptly ended the story. Before he had a chance to ask her about it, their dinner had arrived.

"Can I get you some refills?" the waitress asked as she set their food on the table and took their glasses before they had a chance to answer.

The pizza was hot and steamy as she inhaled the delicious aroma of garlic and oregano. Suddenly ravenous, she dug into the slice of pizza that was still hot from the oven. "Mmm," she cooed, like talking to a baby, "this is just as good as I remember." She closed her eyes and savored the taste that made her mouth water.

"How long do you think you're going to be in town?" Matt asked, taking a big bite of pizza.

"Well, um, I'm not sure," she started, not knowing the answer to that, even though she had asked herself the same question numerous times over the past several days. "I have some vacation and comp time and thought I'd use them and come home for a little visit," she ended dully. How long was she going to be in town? She didn't have a job, a permanent home and was temporarily living in her mother's guest bedroom. Even though she was having a good time and enjoying her visit, it couldn't go on forever. She had to get back to the real world.

Later that night after he dropped her off, Matt headed back home, unable to shake Jillian Simmons from his mind. It had been such a shock to see her at the game. He didn't even know she was in town, yet he was glad to see her. He fleetingly thought about her over the years. She still looked the same, he thought. She looked as though she hadn't aged on bit. Her hair was still long and dark, her eyes were still the same chocolate brown that had melted his heart when she'd fixed them upon him. She probably wasn't aware when she did it, which made her even more sexy and hard to resist. Certainly, her body was still incredible and shapely. But she'd filled out, adding womanly curves to a figure that could stop traffic, not to mention the long, shapely legs he couldn't seem to take his eyes off as she walked in front of him. He waited until she got into her mom's house to make sure she was safe, or so he had told himself. It had just been for the sheer pleasure of watching her walk, her hips swaying slightly and seductively. Yes, Jillian Simmons was a beautiful, sexy woman, and she had just walked back into his life. Things were going to get complicated, he thought with a smile.

Unable to fall asleep, Jillian grabbed one of books from her nightstand to help her brain slow down and find sleep.

Most of her books were still at Kevin's, so she borrowed a paperback from her mom. She snuggled down into bed, losing herself in the story before drifting off to sleep.

CHAPTER 18

They were walking barefoot on the beach, the wet sand firm beneath their feet as they watched the rise and fall of the surf. It was a gorgeous day, with temperatures in the mid 80's. The breeze off the water was steady and refreshing, cooling the relentless heat of the sun. Seashells dotted the sand as the gray and white gulls splashed around, looking for something to eat. They had woken early after spending a passionate night together. She could feel herself blushing at the thought and smiled in spite of herself. He was wonderful, and she was so glad that she had found him. He knew her so well, she marveled, holding his hand a little tighter for fear of losing him. He turned to look at her, ready to say something, when a ringing sound started.

Shaking her head, she sat upright in bed, dazed and confused. What was she doing in bed, she thought, a second ago she had been walking on the beach with... who had she been walking with? Blinking a few times, she brought herself back to reality and realized her cell phone was ringing. Jumping out of bed, she stubbed her toe on the nightstand and proceeded to curse loudly, using words that would have made a truck driver blush as she grabbed her phone off of the dresser. Seeing Matt again had really had an effect on her.

"Hi, this is Jillian," she answered, automatically using the greeting she had used many times in the past when answering business calls.

"Jillian, where in the world are you?" a loud male voice with a thick southern accent boomed from the other end of the phone. "I called the office and they told me that you don't work there anymore," Rick Colbert stated in a puzzled tone.

Instinctively, she looked for something to put on to cover the gym shorts and t-shirt she had slept in last night. The call had confused her and she forgot that Rick couldn't see her, only hear her. She laughed a little at the thought, then dismissed it and tried to focus on the conversation. She really needed a cup of coffee. It was too early for this. Plus, the dream was still on her mind. She was trying to remember the details. But, like most dreams, it was starting to fade.

"Good morning, Rick. That's right," she began, clearing the sleep from her throat. "I don't work at Williams Consulting anymore." She wasn't sure what information he already knew and didn't want to reveal more than necessary.

"Well, why not? I called there, asked for you and was transferred to Kevin McBride. Personally, I don't trust that man, he's a little too slick for my taste," the Texan commented.

Rick Colbert was a large man with big hands, broad shoulders, and a head full of silver hair. He was tall, at least six foot five, with a menacing appearance; until you got to know him, at least. With a big laugh and an even bigger grin, Rick's personality didn't match his appearance. He was just a nice guy, with a sharp head for business and a quick wit. He inherited the floundering family business when his father passed away and turned it around into a moneymaking machine within two years. The company had been losing money every month due to poor management. But, after he stepped in and took stock of everything, things had started to turn around. Customers were happy once again and Colbert Supply was in the green again. They were in the distribution business, with offices all across the state of Texas and had started branching out to other states. That was where Williams Consulting came in, specifically Jillian. She was the account executive assigned to pitching them with strategies on their expansion. She was focusing on consolidating their operations, as well as analyzing their corporate structure and making recommendations for improvement. Rick had been successful when dealing with a few offices, but the dozen or so they were interested in opening was more than he wanted to handle himself. It was a big step for him to take their business out of Texas and he knew he needed the advice and guidance of a professional.

Her first presentation had gone well as she introduced the services she could provide during the expansion and plans for the next phase of growth. Having succeeded on getting called back for a second meeting, she spent a lot of time organizing and composing presentations on what direction they could take. They had yet to reach an agreement with him, and she figured that was what he was calling about.

"It all happened, um, kind of, uh, suddenly," she stammered, not sure how to explain the situation. Should she just come right out and tell him that she had been fired? It really was confusing, she thought. Then again, maybe that wasn't the best explanation to give a client.

"So, you're not with Williams anymore, is that true?" he asked, not sounding happy. "I have to be honest with you, that doesn't make me happy. You're the first person to come in, analyze our business and propose strategies that actually make sense, will save us money and not cost us a bundle to implement. And you're a pleasure to work with," he ended.

"Don't worry, Rick, I'm sure another account executive will be assigned to handle your account." She wasn't sure why she was defending her former employer who had dismissed her unfairly.

"Frankly, Jillian, I don't want another account executive. I want you and what you brought to the table. The ideas you presented were yours and that's what I want to buy when I sign a contract. I know Kevin whatever contacted me, but I know he didn't have a darn thing to do with the strategies you presented. He could barely explain the high-level strategy and I didn't even ask about the details. He was clueless."

She couldn't help being flattered, but didn't have an answer for him. "I appreciate your vote of confidence and praise, but I'm not in a position to help you anymore."

"Well, what are you doing? Where are you working now? I'll just switch my business to that company and get you back on our team," he stated.

She didn't quite know what to say. On one hand, she was thrilled that he liked her work so much. She had spent a lot of time reviewing his business and thinking of new, innovative ways they could improve. Then again, she didn't have another company to refer him to since she was still unemployed. She was going to have to do something about that, she thought.

"Actually, I'm not working anywhere, Rick. I'm just on vacation."

"So, why not come and work for me? You'd love Texas!" he said, laughing loudly.

She smiled to herself as she pictured his big grin that he flashed often. As interesting as the offer was, she didn't want to move to Texas. "Thanks, Rick. I'm really flattered, but I don't think Texas is for me."

"Yeah, Texas isn't for everyone," he started, still chuckling, "it takes some getting used to. Me, I can't imagine living anywhere else on the planet."

After ending the call, feeling her emotions start to waver, she decided to go for a run and give Ann a call. They'd been missing each other on the phone, but their text game was strong. Since it was a workday, she knew Ann would be bust at her desk.

"Hey Ann," she said, a little out of breath as she warmed up with a light jog.

"Hey yourself," Ann replied, "what're you up to, lounging around, sipping coffee in your jammies?"

"Ha! I wish, I dragged myself out of bed to get in a jog and clear my head. I had an interesting phone call earlier and felt my emotions creeping up, so getting out of the house seemed like the best idea."

"Oh no, don't tell me. Kevin called?"

"No, no," Jillian laughed, "I haven't heard from him. It was one of my most recent clients asking where I was and why I wasn't returning his calls.

"Well that's interesting. I guess Kevin isn't able to fill the hole he created when he ran you out of the company. Good for him. Nice to know that he's feeling your absence. Just hope he's feeling it at home, too."

"Oh, who knows? I'm sure Alexis or someone else is keeping him busy outside of work. I don't really care, but Rick's call made me think about my future a bit. I mean, just because I'm not at Williams, doesn't mean I can't take my skills elsewhere."

"That's my girl! Think outside the box; start throwing around those industry words and lingo. I love it when you talk business to me."

Jillian laughed, "Well, I think I'm in the position now to create the position I want and not have to settle. I have a little bit of savings that will keep me going for a little while. Would it be completely crazy if I opened my own consulting company?" She held her breath, finally saying out loud the words she'd been thinking in the back of her mind for a while. The time had never been right; she didn't have the experience or lengthy client list, but maybe now is the time to start thinking. Stopping to catch her breath, she dropped onto a nearby bench and hydrated with some water from her bottle.

"I think you can do anything you want. You've always had the brain and desire to be successful, but I don't think you had the guts or the time, to be honest. I think you can do it and I think this is the time. It's big for sure, but not out of the question. Sorry to cut you short, hon, but I have to dial-in for a meeting. Love ya girl," she added before disconnecting the call.

Starting the jog back to her mom's, she ran the last part of Rick's conversation through her mind. He had made a lot of sense, and she trusted Rick. Since they started working together, she started picking up on some business tips that she was able to apply to her own work. Learning from a leading business owner in Texas was a bonus. `Rick had a way of commanding respect without bullying the other party, which was more of Kevin's style. Rick issued sincere compliments and had a way of coaching his team about opportunities instead of mistakes. That positive nature earned him the respect he received. Kevin didn't have that soft touch, but that was mostly because of his ego, making him somewhat difficult to work with.

"So, you won't move to Texas, I understand, but I still want you to consult on our expansion. I've told some of my business associates about you and the fine work you've done for us. If you decide you want to open your own business, I can certainly send some work your way."

She had been slightly taken aback by his suggestion, though it had been a nagging thought at the back of her mind here and there. It could be the solution that would allow her to do the work she loved doing, but not have to work about the bureaucracy that went with working for someone else. She could be her own boss, could set-up her business anywhere and work remotely. Technology had definitely advanced over the past several years. A friend of hers told her that their company's remote work policy had changed from "work from home" to "work from anywhere." She could do the work from anywhere, but not the work from home, she laughed to herself. Well, she had to find a home first, she thought, but was suddenly excited about the idea.

"Thanks for the vote of confidence," she had said. "I mean, I'll certainly consider it and let you know," then she had a sinking feeling. She couldn't retain Rick as a client because he was a client of Williams Consulting and she had signed a non-compete agreement. Essentially, the document stated that if she left Williams Consulting, by law, she couldn't work for a competitor or any client retained by Williams Consulting for the period of one year. Well, there goes that, she thought, suddenly deflated. As soon as the carrot had been dangled in front of her, it had been yanked out of her reach. Damn Kevin, she thought!

"Unfortunately, even if I opened my own business, I couldn't retain you as a client, Rick," she explained regretfully. "I signed a non-compete with Williams Consulting. It was a mandatory requirement for all employees."

"A non-compete," he mused, mulling over the thought, "hmm, well, I can see how that would be a problem."

There, that was it. It was over. She stopped picturing her home office and working in her pajamas. That newfound dream wasn't going to turn into a reality.

Rick cleared his throat and continued, "Well, it would be a problem," he repeated, "if I contractually hired Williams Consulting, but I didn't. In fact, the contract is sitting right here on my desk waiting for my signature. And that Kevin McBride is a little too slick for my taste and I'm from oil country, so I know all about slick!" he added with his familiar booming laugh.

109

She was speechless and her heart was racing. It could be done, but could she do it? Even though he hadn't formally hired Williams Consulting, they had done work for him, so it might be tricky. She'd have to consult an attorney. Just add that to her expanding to-do list! She walked into her mother's house and headed to the guest bedroom. Feeling a little lightheaded as the thoughts raced through her mind, she dropped down onto the bed and tried to think of a response. She really needed a professional mentor to help her figure this out. Maybe Rick could help her navigate the next phase of her career.

"I see," she stammered, "so, you aren't actually a client of Williams, which means that the non-compete isn't a factor," she ended smiling. Well, well, she thought, she just might have solved all of her problems. At least some of them, she amended. She could set her own hours. If she wanted to sleep in and start her day at ten in the morning, who was going to stop her? If she was working late into the night, running with a new idea, who was going to tell her the building was closing in five minutes? Nobody, that's who! What a great concept, she thought, getting charged by the idea.

In the end, she thanked Rick again for the call and proposition. She told him she had some things to figure out before she could make any decisions. He said he'd wait a week or two before seeking another RFP for his business, giving her an opening to get back to him and something for her to think about.

After talking to Rick, she suddenly remembered that she hadn't responded to Ryan's text from a few days ago. It slipped her mind and she switched to her messaging app.

"Jillian, Ryan here. Just checking on the final plans. I tried to email you, but it bounced back as undeliverable. Not sure why, but give me a call when you know your flight plans. Enjoyed our recent dinner," he ended with a sexy tone.

Ugh…she had forgotten that she was supposed to fly back out to Ryan's offices and finalize their deal. She had been planning to talk to Betty the week after she returned from her travel to make the next trip's arrangements, but with everything that happened, she had forgotten.

Letting out a big sigh, she figured she might as well text Ryan since she already had Rick Colbert's conversation and offer. There was no way she could continue to work with Ryan since his company's officers had signed their contract with Williams. Her NDA protected that deal for Williams. She had done all of the work and now somebody else would get the glory. Her head was spinning!

CHAPTER 19

Settling into the couch in her mom's family room, Jillian powered up her MacBook and waited for the machine to come to life. Kate had bought a new computer a few years ago after taking a course at the local Apple store. She loved using the machine to keep in touch with her family and friends through e-mail and Facebook Messenger. When traveling, she often booked her reservations online and researched the best values on airfare, often finding terrific deals. Jillian and Jessica had been stunned to receive their first e-mails from their mother; they hadn't even known she knew how to turn on a computer, Jillian she was glad Kate went with a Mac. She'd been a fast learner and often spent evenings, when she was home, online. She recently started watching Netflix and Hulu, sharing tips with her daughters from the latest documentaries and series she'd been watching.

Jillian was an Apple user for life. She loved the connectivity between her devices, the password chain, virus-free environment and vowed to never go back to a PC. Connecting her MacBook to Kate's Wi-Fi, she started browsing.

Exhilarated by the thought of owning her own consulting

business and being her own boss, Jillian wanted to spend some time on research. She really didn't know where to start as a million different thoughts popped in and out of her mind. She needed to think about developing a business plan for the bank, since some sort of financing would definitely be helpful to get started. Then, she had to find somewhere to have her physical office. It was one thing to say that you wanted to work out of your home. But, it was a completely different goal when you didn't have a home to work out of. She needed to slow down and breathe.

A few minutes later, she was deep into her research, browsing Pinterest, LinkedIn and general Google searches. She spent a few minutes reading her e-mail messages. There were quite a few. She hadn't checked her messages since leaving her job and found quite more than a few waiting for her in the two weeks that she had been gone. There were several from her former co-workers, questions about her abrupt departure, the latest gossip and happenings around the office. Jillian chuckled and became nostalgic for the office environment. But, the one that caught her eye was from kmcbride@williams.com and her hand shook as she pulled her hands quickly from the track pad. She couldn't believe what she saw. It was from Kevin. Did she want to open it? She wasn't sure. She checked the date and saw that he had sent it two days ago. Their last encounter had involved her coming home after being fired to find him in a passionate embrace with Alexis, which prompted her to pack her bags and storm out of his house. He hadn't bothered to contact her before and she wasn't sure she wanted to hear what he had to say now. But part of her did. The part that remembered the good times they'd shared, the dinners, vacations, and evenings at home in front of a fire. That Jillian wanted to read what he had to say. The other part of her wanted to just delete the message without even a glance at his words. What could he have to say now that would interest her? She felt weak, with her resolve melting away. They had shared a home and were making a life together, although he'd betrayed her in every way possible.

Taking a deep breath and a glance around, though she was home alone, she clicked on the message and waited for it to appear on the computer screen.

Jillian,

I'm sorry about what happened, but I can't believe that you would blame me. It wasn't my fault that you were let go, and what you saw with Alexis was a mistake. I thought we agreed on moving forward with each other. I want to take you to dinner and talk everything out. We had something good together. I miss you and know you must miss me, too.
Kevin

She read the short message ten times before she could comprehend the words. He didn't think he was to blame? What the hell! It read like a business letter, not an email to your former girlfriend of several years. No closing like sincerely, love, yours truly; Kevin couldn't be bothered. He wanted to get back together with her? What happened with Alexis certainly was a mistake; he was right about that! The mistake was that she found out about them and saw it with her own two eyes. That was the mistake. How dare he say that he didn't have anything to do with her dismissal! He was most certainly the reason she had been fired, and she couldn't believe that he didn't realize that. There was no way, under any circumstances, even if she was starving, that she'd have dinner with him. She was shocked that he'd even written to her, let alone what he had to say in his message. It was just too unbelievable and insane to think that he was that delusional. She knew that Kevin had always been wrapped up in his own life, but this was a bit ridiculous. There wasn't any response that she could send him. She had nothing to say to him and didn't want any further contact.

"He could have called or texted if he wanted to get in touch with me so bad," she muttered to herself, though she might not have answered, knowing he was on the other end of the phone. Sending an email when he wouldn't know when she'd see it was the cowardly way out. And with a click of the mouse, she filed the message in the junk folder and returned to her research.

CHAPTER 20

Stepping onto the front porch, Jillian paused for a minute to take in her surroundings. It was a lovely morning, and she was just starting her jog, though it wasn't even eight o'clock yet. Most weekdays, she would be leaving her hotel room to a customer site, sipping a large coffee to get her through the morning. The thought of not having anything to do all day, nobody to check in with at the office, felt like playing hooky back in school! She felt so carefree and was immediately glad she woke up earlier than she had the last few weeks. Indulging in the extra sleep was part depression and part sheer exhaustion from the non-stop running her career had demanded. These days, she was feeling a little better and more like her old self, pre-Kevin and pre-Williams Consulting.

Unable to sleep, she rose early and headed out, trying not to wake her mom. Outside in the fresh air, she glanced around and was glad she had decided to stay in town a little longer. It felt good to be here, where everything was a little slower and easier than life in the city. She didn't feel rushed or hassled. She laced up her shoes and stepped onto the sidewalk that lined the street.

She'd always loved the small town where she grew up; it

116

was the closeness and comfort that came with living in a place where everyone knew you that she missed.

Deeply inhaling, Jillian filled her lungs with the sweet smell of honeysuckle that wildly wove inside a nice, neat hedge line in one of the yards she passed. After about 10 minutes, she found herself several blocks from Kate's house when she spotted a lovely house set back from the road by about thirty yards. There was a hedge line that bordered the property and she could barely see the house from her vantage point. Something about the surroundings made her want to see more of what was hiding behind the hedges.

The house hidden behind the hedge line was a cute, little bungalow that caught her attention. It looked as though it was vacant - the house was dark and the grass a little high. The tall, stately oak trees that stood in front of the house like soldiers guarding the structure, needed to be trimmed and shaped. Low limbs hung out over the sidewalk in front of the house. Birds chirped and sang out to one another as she moved in a little closer, crouching to avoid the leaves handing low.

From her new vantage point, Jillian could see flowerbeds bordering the front foundation of the house, but it looked as though the flowers and weeds were fighting for space. From her observation, the weeds were winning. Not wanting to trespass, but dying to see more of the house and property, she slowly continued on the sidewalk that led to the front porch, glancing around to be sure that an attack dog wasn't waiting to pounce and chew off her leg Not seeing anybody or hearing anything out of the ordinary, she crept closer to the house.

After peeking through the windows on the ground floor,

117

she wandered around the backyard. The property had a natural hedge fence that hid a charming backyard garden and stone patio from the street view. The garden was overgrown and untended, but she could picture it in her mind as it must have looked when it was cared for and loved. Some perennials were being choked out by the weeds like the flowers in the front, but the hydrangea in the back were showing off their light bluish and purple tones. She thought for a minute why the house wasn't familiar to her since it wasn't far from her childhood home and realized thick trees, hedges and a fence, had surrounded it blocking it from view on the street.

Without knowing more about the property, who owned it, how much the asking price was, she wanted to know more about the house. There was just something about it that made her feel comfortable and homey and she hadn't even seen the inside, just what she was able to glimpse through the dusty windows. Jillian knew that she liked what she saw.

From what she could tell, the house had a living room, dining room, kitchen and sun porch downstairs. Maybe a half bath on the ground floor, too? She guessed there were probably two bedrooms and a bathroom upstairs. Glancing at the For-Sale sign in the front yard, she snapped a quick pic of the realtor's name and number, deciding to call them as soon as they opened.

After agreeing to meet the realtor at the house in an hour, she rushed upstairs to shower and change, thoughts of her new find filling her mind. Over the phone, she had learned a lot from Mary Jane, the realtor. She learned the house needed some work, as the maintenance hadn't been kept up after the previous owner passed away. It sat empty, on and off the market for the past year. A few other people expressed interest, but nothing had come of the inquiries. She's still puzzled that she didn't remember more about the house when she used to live in the neighborhood. Mary Jane told her that the owner of the house was a widower whose wife passed away. He had remodeled to change his surroundings so he wasn't constantly reminded of the love he had lost. He passed away shortly after remodeling and it's sat empty ever since. Nobody in his family had wanted the house and was hoping to get it sold and move on. They were motivated sellers, Mary Jane, confided.

On her way out of the house to meet Mary Jane, she saw Matt walking up the front porch. "Matt, what are you doing here?" Jillian asked, surprised to see him.

"Just dropping by to see if you wanted to get some breakfast."

"I'd love to, but I have an appointment in," she paused to consult her watch, "about 10 minutes, so maybe a rain check? I'm actually meeting a realtor to take a look at a house I saw earlier this morning. It's about 10 minutes away," she continued.

"So, I take it you're planning on staying in town permanently?" he asked, secretly pleased that she was talking about moving back. It would be nice to see her around town again. But, he told himself not to get too ahead of himself. Maybe that wasn't what she wanted.

"Well, I guess so," she laughed, "that is, if the house turns out to be as nice inside as it looks on the outside. I mean, I don't really know, but it's such a great looking property. What do I have to lose by just looking at it? At least that's what I keep telling myself. Now, I guess it needs some work, but it looks good from what I can see." She excitedly told him about the house, asking if he knows the one she's talking about. "I need to slow down, though. Too many things, big things, are happening at the same time.

"I know exactly which house you're talking about. In fact, I remodeled the house for Mr. Peters before he passed away. His wife had died a year before he did and he wanted to change the house, and I got the job. It's a great place and actually, if I remember correctly, it probably doesn't need that much work, just some cleaning, maybe painting." Not wanting to end the conversation, he added, "If you want, I could take a look at it with you. I have some free time this morning."

"Thanks, that would be great!" she enthused, "I mean, if you're sure you're not busy. I don't want to take up your time." She was pleased that he had offered to tag along. He could look at the house from a professional standpoint and let her know what kind of work it would need.

Once there, Jillian found that the house was indeed just as charming inside as she imagined it would be. From the front porch, the door opened into a small entry with hardwood floors, a small closet and a large window, where she envisioned the sun spilling in every morning. A doorway on the right led into the living room where a fireplace sat, surrounded by bookcases on both sides and small windows above the shelves. Glancing around, the room needed a fresh coat of paint, but she pictured her furniture from storage filling the room. She could picture the shelves full of books and some knickknacks from her travels. She could arrange the couch so that it faced the fireplace and the large painting her cousin painted for her over the fireplace. It was a beautiful scene of the pier on

Seneca Lake in New York, a popular destination area with several wineries, cafes, shops and boat docks throughout the mountainous lake area. She nicely captured the scene of a typical day with the boats secured at the dock, people walking the length of the pier, the seagulls riding the gentle waves that lapped at the shoreline, the water gleaming with the rays of the sun shining down. Seeing it made her nostalgic for the relaxing days of wine tastings and late lunches on the lake.

The entry continued into a hallway with a small powder room on the right and the kitchen at the back of the house. Don't get carried away, she reminded herself.

As it turned out, the kitchen was one of Jillian's favorite rooms in the house. She had taken a cooking class in college and wanted to get back to cooking if her scheduled permitted. She wasn't disappointed by what she saw. To the right was a long counter where the refrigerator and pantry had been built in. The left end continued around to the left wall where the oven was located. Looking at the old appliance, she knew she'd have to invest in a new one. A window above the counter looked out onto the stone patio and old flower gardens decorating the backyard. She would set miniature pots of herbs on the windowsill, where they would get plenty of sun throughout the day. An island sat in the middle of the floor, near the counter and appliances. The island hid a small dishwasher and several deep drawers, with a sink on top. The walls were covered with white wallpaper that featured an ivy pattern, coordinating with the light-colored cabinets. The wallpaper wasn't her style, and she made a mental note to ask about renting a steamer from the hardware store.

French doors off the kitchen led to the patio where she could picture her gas grill. Jillian would definitely have to buy some patio furniture, she thought with a smile of anticipation and enthusiasm.

To the left of the kitchen, the sunroom was large, bright and airy. She could imagine sitting in this room in the morning, enjoying a leisurely cup of coffee while reading the newspaper. As she looked out the sun porch windows, Jillian thought her eyes were deceiving her, so she leaned in closer and squinted her eyes. Out in the backyard, just off of the patio, she saw two big, old, sturdy trees that were spaced about ten feet apart. She could barely contain her excitement and Matt noticed her expression.

"Jilly, what is it?" he asked, wondering what was causing her big smile.

"Look out there," she said; her voice barely above a whisper as she pointed to what had captured her attention. "Those trees are just close enough for a hammock to be hung between them. I've always wanted a hammock," she ended with a sigh. She was meant to own this house, now she knew that for certain.

"Shall we head upstairs?" Mary Jane asked from the kitchen. In her excitement, Jillian had forgotten she was there and gave a little noise of surprise when she spoke.

On the second floor, there were two bedrooms and a full bathroom, as she had guessed from outside. The smaller of the two bedrooms had two large windows that faced the front street. A spacious closet was situated to the left of the door as you entered the room. She could see that Mr. Peters had stopped the renovations on the first floor. Both bedrooms needed to be updated and refreshed. One had been painted a light aloe green that was soft and soothing. The hardwood floors looked ok, but she'd have to ask

Matt later. As she walked around the rooms, surveying the space, the sound of her shoes echoed slightly in the empty space.

Across the hall, the room was larger, but afforded the same coziness. A skylight and two windows made the room bright, especially in the early morning sun. Years ago, she'd splurged on a sleigh bed. It was a lovely piece of furniture that she'd covered with a hand-sewn antique quilt her grandmother had made for her when she lived in her own apartment. She could picture her bed, the matching dresser, chest of drawers arranged neatly in the large room. She already felt at home here. Sliding open the doors of the closet, she could see the dust and cobwebs that had moved into the empty space.

Before the tour was finished and the price discussed, she had decided that she had to buy the house. There was no question about it, not a shadow of doubt in her mind as she listened to Mary Jane's sales pitch. She was half-tempted to tell her that she could stop with the speech; the house was sold. She was startled by the quickness of her decision, but didn't question it, knowing it was the right thing to do. Her mind was going in a million different directions, as the endless possibilities continued. But, a gut feeling wasn't something to be ignored!

She'd missed too much of what was important in life by worrying about work, Kevin, business trips, and events for work. When you're in it, she thought, you couldn't see outside of it, so she hadn't realized how much her life had changed. She wanted to live life at a slower pace and realized how much she missed her hometown. If she became her own boss, she would be able to set the pace and the schedule for her work.

Spending time with her family had reminded her of the things that she had been missing. She missed the slow pace of living in a small town. Small towns were definitely different than the city, obviously, but even more so, the suburbs outside of a large city were equally different. The people, the vibe of the area, the landscape, everything was different. Jillian had to admit that she missed living somewhere where most everybody knew everyone else. It was kind of comforting, in fact, to live in that kind of environment. There was a strong sense of home and community in a small town. She could remember how each summer there was a huge summer picnic for everyone in town at the park near the lake. Booths were set-up with a variety of carnival-like games, cotton candy, funnel cakes, craft sales, and flea markets. A band played oldies and she remembered dancing with her dad, a memory she held closely to her heart. Her family had never missed one while she and Jessica were growing up. Everyone in the town pulled together to make the weekend a success. It was a point of pride on Sunday night when the closing parade made its way through the neighborhood surrounding the lake. If she closed her eyes and concentrated hard enough, she could still picture the scene as if it was yesterday. Things like that had been missing from her life for so long, that she'd forgotten about them. That is, until Jillian had come home. Being with her family had changed her. Thoughts of Kevin didn't clog her mind 24/7, though she hadn't completely shaken him. She had a lot to look forward to and she was ready to plunge forward, making changes in her life that made her happy.

She did pause, though, with her emotions running so high to stop and think about moving forward and if it was the right move. She'd been letting her emotions dictate her moves and her mind. Did she want to return to her hometown? Was that a sign of defeat, of giving in, of failing? Was it failure to come running back to her family, given everything that happened?

With any family, you never see everything or the whole picture all at once. Sometimes you never see it at all. She thought about her family and how they tended to reveal their secrets slowly, like a whisper. And if you didn't listen close enough, you might miss it all together. Should she really move home? She could always return to the city and find another job, or she could move to a new city where she was anonymous and start a new job. Starting over was like shedding an old suit, she thought. Did she want the brand-new suit that came with a new city or did she want to pull an old comfortable one from the back of her closet and see if it still fit?

Matt sensed a change in her. He couldn't quite put his finger on it and wasn't able to read her like he used to be able to. But, there was something different about her. She seemed as though a weight had settled in on her. Earlier it seemed like she was freer, but now she seemed more inside herself.

"Do you want to get that coffee?" she asked him, suddenly turning toward him with a slight grin, as though she'd made a sudden decision.

"So, what are you thinking?" Matt inquired, stealing a sideways glance at her as they stopped at the corner, waiting to cross the street. She really looked terrific this morning. With her hair pulled back into a ponytail and a flush in her cheeks, she looked as though she was a college freshman heading to a football game. He still couldn't believe she was back in town. If her reaction to seeing the house was any indication, he had a feeling she was here to stay. He liked that.

"I'm thinking," she paused, turning to look at him with a serious expression, "that I'm going to be a homeowner soon," she ended with a grin. "I mean, Matt, as I walked around the house I could just picture living there," she explained, the words coming faster as her excitement continued to mount. "I could see how I'd arrange my furniture, decorate the living room. It's just so perfect, but am I ready to be a homeowner? Am I ready to quit and come back home? Is that what fate is telling me to do?"

Sipping their drinks, they settled outside at a café table to enjoy the sun. She continued her heavy thinking and listened to him talk about the changes in town.

"Mmm…" she hummed, closing her eyes, enjoying the strong coffee and delicate foam on her cappuccino.

"Yeah, this place opened a few years ago and has been pretty popular ever since," Matt explained, shielding his eyes from the sun. "I try to support as many local businesses as I can, but this is one of my favorites. That's the thing about a small town, you really do get to know everyone and have a strong sense of community. Being a small business owner myself, I know the importance of networking and staying loyal. So many of these businesses have contracted with me to do small jobs that may stay small or may end up being bigger and more involved, but delivering good service and quality work is what I aim for."

"I know what you mean," she paused, "in the city or even the suburbs, you don't always get a sense of community. It's the smaller towns where you feel the nostalgia and see generations of families who continue to plant roots where they grew up. I like that. I always thought the fast pace of city life was for me, and don't get me wrong, I love the city. But the past few weeks, slowing down has been good for me. I've been forced to take a look at my life and priorities. My path is changing, and I think I'm ready for that, but it's scary."

Jillian stood up as she finished her sentence, laughing out loud as Matt grabbed her up in a quick hug, easily lifting her off her feet and twirling her around before setting her back down on the sidewalk. Laughing and smiling, they stared at each other, slightly breathless from the movement, though it only lasted a few seconds. Running a hand through her hair, she tried to calm herself down, but her heart was racing so fast, she swore it would beat right out of her chest. Matt still had the same effect on her that he did in high school. He could get her excited and very passionate without much effort. Sexy was definitely a word to describe him, especially this morning. He was dressed in a pair of soft, faded denim Levis that were slightly snug. His tight black t-shirt showed-off his well-developed biceps that flexed under his skin whenever he moved. She just wanted to reach out and squeeze his arm to feel his strength. But, somehow, she managed to control herself, until she looked into his eyes. He was staring down at her with such smoldering intensity; she felt her breath catch in her throat. Without thinking, she instinctively stepped into his arms as he pulled her in close to him. He never broke eye contact, his blue eyes deep and sensual. They were standing chest to chest, without a hint of space or air between them. She was quivering slightly with anticipation of what was to come. His breathing was heavy, the scent of his cologne faint. Being this close to him, this intimate, made her moan out loud as he slowly brought his mouth down to hers. The first kiss was tender, his soft lips barely brushing hers, just a hint of a kiss that simmered with passion. She wound her arms around his neck and pulled

127

him in closer, running her hands through his hair as the first kiss turned into another, growing more passionate. Jillian could feel the heat of his body as Matt rubbed his hands up and down her back, his strong, firm hands slowly caressing the skin of her bare arms before they settled on her waist, his thumbs barely brushing the sides of her breasts. Stepping a little closer, she turned her head slightly, giving him easier access to her full, waiting mouth. She completely gave herself up to the moment, kissing him with the pent-up passion that had been lacking in her life. Just as quickly as the kiss started, he pulled away from her, staring at her, trying to catch his breath.

"Jillian," he whispered as the sound of an approaching car jolted them back to reality and the present. With a start, he looked around, temporarily forgetting where they were. "I'm sorry, I shouldn't have done that," he ended, his voice deep, husky and full of smoldering passion from the intense moment. With a sigh of regret, he ran a hand through his thick dark hair, as though he didn't know how the kiss had started.

"Uh, that's ok," she said lamely, not knowing what else to say. She'd been too caught up in the kiss that had rocked her world to care about the consequences. For that brief moment, she'd let her body guide her mind, not the other way around. And, she admitted to herself, it felt good. For once, she got out of her own head and the constant spiral of thoughts about what to do.

CHAPTER 21

Back at home, Jillian could barely contain her excitement about the house and her impromptu coffee date with Matt. She smiled at the thought of how wonderful it felt to be in his arms again, but she wasn't reading too much in to the moment. It was a one-time kiss that was bound to happen sooner or later, she decided. They would both forget about it. With that out of the way, they could get on with being friends again. She wasn't going to run into someone's arms on the rebound from Kevin. Plus, Matt had only kissed her, not proposed marriage. It wasn't like she hadn't enjoyed the moment spent in his arms. They were nice arms, she thought with a laugh, as was everything else about him. But, they were both grown-ups and not high school kids anymore. She needed to act like the adult she was.

He'd certainly grown up well. She couldn't help but notice just how sexy he really way. It surprised her that he was still single. She wouldn't let things get carried away. But, her visit had put them in contact. Being back in town was sure to make that contact more frequent, especially if she was going to relocate. He had already offered to give her an estimate on the work that needed to be done to make the house ready for her to move in. Naturally, she'd hire him to do the remodeling and maintenance work needed on the house - not that it needed much work. It wouldn't make sense to get bids from other contractors when she already knew and trusted Matt.

Now that she had found a terrific house, she was seriously contemplating moving home. It wouldn't be that big of a deal. She was already here, and it felt like home to her again. It was simply a matter of moving the rest of her belongings. A one-day trip to her storage unit in the city would be enough time to pack everything and drive moving truck back from the city. She was sure she could enlist Jessica and Jack to help, and she knew Ann would be up for the adventure. But, she wouldn't do that until she closed on the house and had it all ready to go. Actually, the first step should be securing financing and offering a fair bid on the house. Just the thought of the house made her smile. It would be a place to call her own, her own space to decorate and furnish how she wanted. Without a steady stream of income, though, could she even get a mortgage? She'd have to call Jack and find out.

Finally settling that there was nothing waiting for her in the city; no job, no house to sell or try to rent, no relationship to consider. She was her own person, free to do whatever was going to make her happy. Actually, it was a pretty good position to be in, she thought.

Her mom wasn't home from the store, yet, so she couldn't share her good news with her. She hadn't even had a chance to tell Jessica about the call from Rick Colbert or the house, let alone the encounter with Matt. But, it was probably best to keep that tidbit to herself, or Jessica would be planning her wedding already!

CHAPTER 22

A few days later, Jillian was surveying the refrigerator in hopes of a snack. Her breakfast had consisted of a blueberry muffin her mother had baked the previous night with a large glass of ice-cold milk. In her opinion, milk could only be enjoyed if it was extremely cold - unless it was in a cappuccino, of course. There were more muffins, but she wanted something more substantial than that. Deciding to make a turkey sandwich, she started gathering what she needed from the refrigerator before heading to the island in the center of the kitchen. A few minutes later, the phone rang. Since it was Saturday morning, she figured her sister was calling to make plans for the day.

"Hello," she said, picking up the phone, juggling a jar of mayonnaise and a tomato.

"Jilly, is that you?" a male voice asked. Only a few people called her Jilly anymore. It was Matt, not Jessica, on the phone. Her stomach did a little flip flop as she instantly recognized the deep, sexy voice on the other end of the phone. This was turning out to be a pretty good day, she thought with a smile. She couldn't help but smile at the delight she felt from him.

"Uh, yeah it's me. Hi, Matt."

"Are you busy? I could use some help and thought of you. Could you lend a hand with a little project I have to get done today? I can pick you up in about fifteen minutes, ok?"

"A project? What do you mean? How can I help you? I don't know the first thing about construction, Matt," she laughed, though she was excited about the prospect of seeing him.

Jillian found herself thinking about him more and more lately. They were happy thoughts, and for once, she felt like just letting go and giving herself up to the moment. She'd been so serious for so long and it was rather exhausting, not to mention lonely. Nobody should have so many rules for themselves, she thought, warming up to the idea of helping Matt. Frankly, it didn't matter to her what he needed help with. She just wanted to see him again.

"Well, what should I wear?" she asked, hurriedly putting everything for her sandwich back in the refrigerator. Her growling stomach would just have to wait a little bit longer, she decided, and ran upstairs to change her clothes.

Fifteen minutes later, Matt pulled into her mother's driveway in his Jeep. Dark aviator shades shielded his eyes, so she couldn't see that he was staring right into her eyes, though she could sense it. She had just finished changing into casual denim shorts, a white t-shirt and her tennis shoes. He'd been specific about the shoes, which only increased her interest in this project of his. He was an intriguing person and she trusted him completely, no matter how many years had passed between them.

132

"Hi," she called from the porch. "Can I bring anything with me?"

"Just yourself," he said with a grin as he walked around to open the passenger's door for her. "Bye, Kate," he called to Jillian's mother who was weeding her flower garden on the side of the house.

"Have fun, kids," Kate smiled and waved. She was glad to see Jillian smiling again.

"So, what's this mysterious project?" Jillian asked as Matt pulled out of the driveway and headed down the road.

"You'll see in a few minutes," he teased with a lazy grin. "Hey, no peeking," he admonished as she turned to look in the backseat for clues. She smiled her sweet smile that melted his heart, making him glad that he had worked up the courage to call her.

It had been risky, but he decided that it was worth it, stealing a glance at her. After all, they'd already had one date. Well, actually they had two dates; pizza after the ballgame was the first. Then, if you counted looking at the house she wanted to buy, that was date number two. Plus, there was that incredibly mind-blowing kiss after seeing the house. It was amazing that something as innocent as a kiss could send his blood pressure shooting through the roof. Then again, it wasn't just any kiss; it was a kiss with Jillian, who'd always been able to get him excited without much effort. She just had that effect on people - on men. But, it was as if she wasn't even aware of her incredible sex appeal. He sure was.

They chatted easily on the drive. Conversation flowed without much effort, adding a nice, comfortable rhythm to the drive. There was something about being together with her, he decided, that reminded him of coming home. Maybe it was the way that she knew him so well. It had been a long time, but she still knew so many personal, intimate details about the kind of person he was, and that was comforting. He would be content to just spend the whole day with her, catching up on the past, finding out more about the woman she had become. The gorgeous, sensual, captivating woman she had become, he corrected. Actually, he wouldn't mind catching up and talking while tangled up together between the sheets of his bed. After their kiss earlier in the day, feeling the passion that was just simmering below the surface, he could only imagine how mind-blowing an afternoon in bed would be. Feeling himself becoming aroused at the prospect, he refocused on driving, staring at the green trees, willing his blood pressure - and the other pressures that became intense - to settle down.

Before long, Matt was easing the Jeep into a parking place in the large lot that serviced the public park on the edge of town, near the northern end of the lake. It was a beautifully scenic recreation spot that was a favorite weekend retreat for everyone in the area. With a long, walking/biking trail, waterfalls, rock-climbing hills and picnic areas, the lakefront park was usually crowded most weekends in the summer. Today, the beach was especially crowded since temperatures were in the eighties and there wasn't a cloud in the sky.

Jillian remembered coming here in the summer with her family. She and Jessica had loved swimming with their father, enjoying the relaxing ease of the little vacations, as they used to call the trips, though they lived so close. It had been fun and the memories brought a smile to her face.

"So, this was your project, Matt?" she asked as he unloaded the wicker picnic basket that had belonged to his mother. Jillian was smiling and apparently not at all upset that he'd tricked her into spending the afternoon picnicking with him.

Matt just smiled broadly in reply to her question. It pleased him that she was smiling and laughing. Even though he told himself that she wouldn't be upset that he had tricked her, he was still a little nervous. Her obvious delight, however, told him that there had been nothing to worry about.

Without a clue as to what you took on a picnic, he had called Susan earlier in the day. His resourceful sister had come through and delivered the basket full of food. He added a small cooler with a couple cans of pop and a bottle of chilled wine and glasses. Susan had even added a picnic blanket. She had asked who his guest was, but he hadn't told her, much to her annoyance. He didn't want to talk about Jillian yet. Who knew what was going to happen? It was foolish of him to start thinking about her so seriously, but he just couldn't get her out of his mind.

They walked for a while, until they had found the perfect spot for an intimate picnic. They were on top of a small hill with a breathtaking view of the lake, beach and some of the waterfalls from the nearby rock formations. A large, stately oak tree lent some shade from the hot sun, and they eagerly dug into the delicious food Susan had packed. Both were hungrier than they had thought.

"I can't believe you did all this, Matt," Jillian remarked when she saw him pull one container after another out of the basket. After arranging everything, he handed her a plate and silverware and told her to help herself.

"I have to confess that I had some help from my sister. You remember Susan, don't you?"

"Sure, I remember her, and I definitely owe her a thank you for this potato salad; it's wonderful."

In addition to the potato salad, there was a loaf of soft French bread, cheese, fruit salad, thin slices of honey ham, homemade chocolate chip cookies, pasta salad and the sweetest cherry tomatoes she had tasted in a long time. She had forgotten how delicious home-grown vegetables were. It was a feast fit for a king, she decided, and dug in heartily.

For a while, they ate in companionable silence, enjoying the food, good company and gorgeous day. The sun was shining high above with a few clouds bouncing about in the gentle breeze. From the beach below, they could hear the laughter from the group of kids frolicking around in the water. The beachfront area was packed as families had their beach blankets spread out, just above the reach of the gently lapping waves that brushed along the shore. Colorful umbrellas were planted in the sand, providing shade from the warm rays of the sun.

"Matt, thanks so much for this," Jillian said, gesturing to everything around her. "You have no idea how much I needed a carefree afternoon."

That was interesting, he thought, as he smiled and nodded in her direction. It seemed like she was ready to talk and he was curious about what had brought her back home.

"So, I take it that you haven't gone on a picnic in a long

time. What happened, Jillian?" he asked in a soft gentle voice.

For a long time, she didn't answer him, wanting to choose her words carefully. She took a sip of the sweet, chilled wine while gathering her thoughts. It was a lot to tell someone you hadn't seen in ten years, she thought. But, it was Matt, not some stranger she had just met. He knew her and she knew him. They had always been comfortable confiding in each other, so she decided to plunge ahead.

"I'm not sure where to start," she confessed, playing with the cuff on her denim shorts, avoiding his eye.

"How about at the beginning?" he suggested quietly, knowing that she needed time. "What brought you back home?"
"I lost my job," she stated simply. "I was let go from my job, lost my boyfriend, my home, all in one day," she said with a rueful laugh. It still sounded absurd, even to her, the person who had lived through the life changing experience. "It's kind of a long story," she said, almost apologetically.

"I'm not going anywhere, if you want to talk about it," he offered.

So, she told him. She told him everything, not leaving out any details. Sharing her feelings and the hurt she had felt was hard, but in a way, she also found it cleansing. It was if she was finally putting the story to rest and leaving the past where it belonged, in the past. The hardest part, the part where she felt like a failure was telling Matt, a man she was interested in romantically, about how she had found about Kevin and Alexis's affair. It was hard to admit that she must have not been a good enough companion, lover, confidante, since Kevin had sought out a relationship outside of theirs. She felt like a failure.

"Jillian, look at me," Matt said, holding her soft, delicate hands in his strong grasp. "You didn't do anything wrong. You have nothing to feel sorry about.

It wasn't your fault that your jerk boyfriend got you fired because he couldn't satisfy you. He wasn't good enough for you and he figured that out.

"Matt, don't you see? I failed! I couldn't hold onto my job, my house, or my boyfriend. I lost everything!"

"You didn't fail, Jillian. You were too good for him, he knew that, but you need to see that for yourself. You're better than this Kevin guy could ever dream of being, and that's what he figured out before you did. Coming home was the best thing for you to do," he added, kissing her hand gently.

"Thanks, Matt," she said softly.

Reaching over, he brushed away a strand of hair that had fallen in her eyes. It was a sweet, gentle gesture that made her realize everything that had been missing in her relationship with Kevin. He never did things like that.
Seeing the intense, smoldering look in his eyes, she slowly got to her knees and   crawled across the short distance that separated them on the blanket.   Not breaking eye contact with him, she sat down next to him, sitting hip to hip with him. He was staring at her intently as he leaned in toward her, sheltering her in the warmth and strength of his embrace. That was exactly where she wanted to be.

"Jillian," he whispered, his voice husky as his lips hovered an inch above hers. "It is so nice to see you again," he said, before bringing his lips down to her.

CHAPTER 23

On Monday morning, Jillian found herself walking into the downtown offices of First Bank and Trust, pulling on her sunglasses to shade the sun from her eyes as she glanced around the town. It was a historic building in the middle of town, with large concrete columns that reached from ground level to the second story. An impressive structure that had been featured in countless historic publications about their area, the bank had recently been renovated back to its original splendor. The interior of the first floor housed twelve teller windows along both sides of the building. Offices for the loan department, new account services and customer service were arranged comfortably along the left wall. She remembered visiting the bank with her mother when she was younger. The tellers always had baskets of candy for kids. Her favorites were the orange lollipops, and she made sure she always got one before they left the bank. Jessica preferred purple. They giggled as they stuck colored tongues out at each other in the car. So many memories of living in a small, rural town had her smiling in spite of herself.

"Good morning," she said to the bank employee at the desk, "I was hoping to meet with Jack Mason, if he has time this morning," she added, hoping her brother-in-law had time to see her.

She'd gone to the bank on impulse, Rick Colbert's call on her mind. She was seriously thinking about starting her own consulting company and had a good chance at success. With that energy vibrating through her and her mind buzzing with questions, she needed to find out about financing options for her potential business.

"Jillian?" the employee inquired over the top of her thick, round glasses, "Is that you? Jillian Simmons?" The chubby woman was grinning from ear to ear, but Jillian was dumbfounded. Did she know this person? She didn't look familiar, but it had been so long since she had been home long enough to go to the bank. But, this lady looked too young to have worked here when she was growing up.

"Uh, yes," she said tentatively with a smile, "that's me, Jillian Simmons."

"It's me! Betsy Smith!" Don't you remember? We had eleventh grade English together with that boring, old Mr. Fitzpatrick. Gosh, you look terrific!" Betsy added as she quickly came around from behind her desk to greet Jillian with a huge hug.

Jillian was taken aback by the gesture, but didn't have a chance to move out of the way as Betsy hugged her with a grin like she had just won the lottery. I don't even remember this person, she thought, but couldn't let the hugging woman know.

"Oh yes," she stammered, "he was such a bore," she added with a laugh.

"Jillian, what a nice surprise," Jack said slowly guiding her away from Betsy's desk, much to the latter's disappointment.

"Nice to see you, Jillian, let's grab a coffee sometime," Betsy waved as Jillian smiled and waved.

"This is a nice surprise visit. What can I do for you?" Jack asked once they were settled in his comfortable office. Jillian surveyed her surroundings and found that Jack's office suited him perfectly. There were framed pictures of Daniel and Hannah on the cherry wood credenza behind the massive cherry wood desk. His office had a comfortable, homey vibe that probably made customers feel at ease when discussing their financial affairs with him.

"Well, I have a couple of questions," she began, taking a deep breath before continuing, "about starting my own business. It would be a consulting business that I would open in my home. I don't know much about running a business, you know, the behind the scenes stuff. I know how to consult and make organizational plans, but it's the managing a business that I haven't done before. I don't know enough about financing, taxes, insurance, day-to-day management and thought you could help guide me until I get my feet wet."

"Well that's a lot more than I thought you wanted to talk about. I thought you wanted to take out a personal loan or something to help while you're out of work and here you want wanting to know about opening your own business."

"If you don't have time," she began, but he cut her off.

"Jillian, how long have I known you? Have I ever not had time to answer any of your questions?" Jack asked with a grin.

"No," she admitted sheepishly, "but…"

"But nothing. Now let's start at the beginning and talk about your options, and then you can buy me lunch."

She laughed in response, agreeing to his terms. From there, they discussed all of the services the bank could offer her for securing a mortgage, small business loan, small business line of credit and other options. Jack's knowledge in the finance industry was exactly what Jillian needed. It reassured her that this was something she could do. She was proud of herself and left with disclosures, account agreements and confidence. She even kept her end of the bargain and took Jack out for a burger at the shop across the street from the bank. It had been quite an eventful morning and she drove home feeling like she had really accomplished something. She was on her way to becoming her own person and she couldn't wait to see where she landed next.

After talking through the options, she decided to open her company as a limited liability corporation. Jack shared the pros and cons of each business structure, but encouraged her to consult with an attorney and accountant before making her final decision. The LLC would give her personal protection from any potential lawsuits she was faced with - heaven forbid, she thought. And it was a simple structure that she could manage independently without much outside help. In the beginning, she thought that adding staff wasn't a priority, but she thought maybe a secretary would be nice to help with errands, copying and other tasks that would distract her from securing deals and working with clients. Those were her priorities as far as she could see.

Also, she knew enough about expense accounts and could learn what she didn't know about office overhead and other costs to maximize her capital. She chuckled thinking that she might know what she's talking about!

CHAPTER 24

"Hello," Jillian answered after the second ring.

"Hey Jillian," Matt said

"Oh hey, Matt."

She felt herself blush, as though he had caught her thinking about their picnic a few days ago. It was as if he knew that she had been replaying the scene in her mind. But, it had been nearly a week since she'd talked to him. She'd been busy planning her business and trying to learn everything she needed to know.

"I was just thinking that, ah," Matt paused, as if he had lost his train of thought, "I was thinking that you'd like to have dinner with me tonight. That is, if you don't already have other plans," he added.

Damn it, he thought! He wasn't asking her to spend the rest of her life with him; it was just an invitation to dinner. Not like they hadn't just shared a pizza and a picnic over the past few weeks. Why was he so nervous about that? This was Jillian, someone he knew and not a stranger he had just met. But that was also part of the problem. This was Jillian, someone he had spent many compromising situations with, not someone he didn't know. He figured he probably knew her better than anyone, including the jerk she had dated in the city.

Here it was, she thought, the dinner invitation. If she accepted this, she knew she was opening herself up to him and inviting further situations with him. There was no doubt that she was still attracted to him. That had been determined during their picnic. After eating, they had entertained themselves with long kisses and passionate embraces under the hot rays of the bright sun. There was something about kissing in broad daylight that seemed so incredibly decadent. The sheer abandon she had felt in his arms was enough to make her stop and think about how she should handle Matt in the future. Obviously, he was still interested in her, but could they go back to being so close without destroying the friendship they were rebuilding? She wasn't sure, given the heat of the moments they shared. But, then again, maybe it was just a dinner invitation with no strings attached. She scolded herself for reading too much into it and jumping to conclusions without any proof.

"What did you have in mind?" she asked, stalling for time. She wasn't sure what to do. Her mind was telling her to decline, but her body and emotions were ready to jump through the phone and into his arms again. What was wrong with her! She had completely lost her mind, she thought.

"Well, nothing too fancy. Just dinner," he paused. "That's ok, I'm sure you're busy," he ended, sounding annoyed.

Before she could think about her answer anymore, she

blurted, "I can be ready around 6:00, if that's ok with you."

After hanging up the phone, he popped the top off of the beer bottle, took a long, healthy swallow and contemplated his actions. He never should have called, he thought, disgusted with himself. She probably only said yes out of pity for him. He was such an idiot. Jillian was a city girl and had only been home for a few weeks. He'd nearly lost his mind when he saw her at the softball game. Pushing her would ruin things and that was the last thing he wanted. There were enough complications without this. Time and distance had drawn them apart before.

Now she was back. It was like fate had changed its mind and dropped her in the middle of his life. There were things he needed to tell her that she should probably hear sooner rather than later. He was walking a tight rope that could collapse beneath him at any moment, but where Jillian was concerned, he was unable to hold back the feelings that had always been there, even when she wasn't. He would tell her tonight, he decided. It wasn't worth risking her friendship, since that might be all this is.

CHAPTER 25

"Hello?" Jessica called through the screen door on the front porch, "Anyone home?" She had been out running errands and wanted to enjoy a visit with her mom and sister without the kids, a rare occurrence. Hannah and Daniel loved their aunt and enjoyed spending time with her whenever they could. Having Jillian back home had been great for all of them. She hoped her sister had found something here that she'd been missing and would decide to stay. In the short time Jillian had been back, Jessica sensed calmness in her that she hadn't seen in her older sister in a long time.

"Hey Jessie," Jillian called, walking from the kitchen to unlatch the door for her sister. Looking behind Jessica as she walked in the room, she asked in a surprised tone, "Are you alone? Where are the kids?" It was rare to see Jessica without at least one of her kids attached to her hip. It seemed like Jessica had been born to be a mother, while Jillian had opted for the career woman route. Had it been a wise choice at the fork in the road? She had been wondering that a lot lately.

"They're at home with Jack. I was out running errands and thought I'd pop in for a bit," she explained, taking the glass of lemonade from Jillian's outstretched hand and helping herself to a long drink. "Thanks, it's hot out there."

"Well, come on into the family room. Mom's not here. I was just getting a drink and doing some research online."

The family room was the part of the addition their father had added when they'd been in grade school. It was a comfortable, cozy room that ran the length of the house with a fireplace, matching sofas and a flat screen TV nearly as big as a movie screen the girls had bought Kate for Christmas a few years earlier. She loved it, but had admonished the girls for spending so much money on her. Now, she enjoyed spending evenings streaming movies or shows.

The relaxing room included a large picture window that faced the front street, while French doors at the other end led to the patio out back. The room was comfortably furnished to match the rest of the house. Kate had adopted a simple design style that focused on casual comfort - like a seaside cottage. The room was painted a light gray with most of the color coming from the richly shaded throw pillows for a pop of color, as Kate had begun saying after watching so much HGTV. Several paintings from local artists adorned the walls as trinkets were arranged on some of the surfaces. Kate loved to browse thrift shops, a trait her girls had acquired from her.

Growing up, they spent a lot time in this room doing homework, watching movies and playing games with their friends or hanging out with their parents after dinner. A lot of great memories had been made here. Jillian could remember slumber parties with her friends from school. Their sleeping bags would be scattered in front of the fireplace and TV. They'd stay up for hours giggling, talking about boys, school, their dreams, everything on the minds of pre-teen girls. Clinging to one another with their eyes hidden, they used to watch the scary movies Jillian and Jessica had in their DVD queue, though they'd have nightmares for weeks after the party.

The sisters settled into the opposite couches, stretching out and relaxing with their drinks. The ceiling fan stirred the air, making the room a comfortable retreat from the oppressive heat and humidity outside. Sounds of kids playing and riding bikes outside mixed with the birds tweeting to one another in the trees outside. It was a typical summer day in the small town and Jillian had been enjoying the relaxing atmosphere, lost in her thoughts of the past few days' events. Without trying, she had been pretty busy on many different levels in her life. She had re-connected with her ex high school boyfriend, been offered a job with a former client, encouraged to open her own consulting business, found her dream house and discussed loan options for her house and business. It had been a whirlwind, and she had stopped thinking about Kevin so much. He was slowly becoming more and more a thing of the past.

"So, what's been going on? I haven't talked to you much lately," Jessica asked, not acting coy - part of her inquisitive nature. When Jessica had a question, she asked it. She didn't believe in beating around the bush to get the information she wanted. Jillian often thought that Jessica would be a tiger in a business negotiation! But, for now, she's the mama bear to her cubs.

"Well, now that you mention it," Jillian began, "I've had an interesting time lately. I was going to call you and tell you everything, but it's been happening pretty quickly. I haven't had a chance to tell Mom about it. She's been busy with work, her committees and friends. She wears me out just watching her!"

"Yeah, mom keeps busy. She loves watching the kids, but sometimes her schedule is so packed that we call in a back-up babysitter. Enough about mom, don't keep me in suspense!" Jessica said impatiently, "Wait, let me guess. Matt jumped your bones and you've been his sex slave at his house?" she asked giggling and dodging the pillow Jillian aimed at her head. Jessica was talking about their dinner after the softball game. She didn't even know about their picnic or coffee or house hunting, though she was sure their mother had told her that she had left with Matt. But Jillian hadn't told anyone how enjoyable the picnic had been. After all, there were some things, like kissing and rolling around in the grass, that you just kept to yourself!

"Jessica!" Jillian laughed, "Come on, be serious. Nothing happened between us that night," she said, which wasn't exactly a lie. It hadn't happened that night, it had happened on the sidewalk after seeing the house and during their picnic. Maybe she'd tell her that part later.

"Alright, so tell me what's going on. I'll behave," Jessica teased by crossing her heart.

"Well, let me see, where should I begin? Ok, do you remember my last business trip? The one to Texas?"

"Umm…yeah, that was right before you came home, right?"

"Yep, that's the one. Anyway, the client I was visiting is named Rick Colbert and he runs his family business that's been around for generations. Anyway, he has offices throughout Texas, but now he wants to branch out into other states that he's targeted as potential markets. He wants to expand his business's footprint," she paused to make sure Jessica was still paying attention. Jillian knew she could get carried away on a topic she was intimate with and passionate about.

"So, he called me the other morning. To make a long story short, he called me at the office, found out that I didn't work there anymore, he was mad because Kevin had been assigned as my replacement and he doesn't like Kevin. So, he called me on my cellphone to find out why I didn't work there and why I wasn't going to be his account executive anymore. Without going into too much detail, I told him the story, keeping out the personal parts. He offered to pull his business from Williams, where he hadn't yet signed a contract, move me to Texas and give me a job in the company," she smiled as Jessica shook her head at that thought. She wasn't thrilled at the notion of Jillian moving to Texas either. "Or," Jillian continued, pausing dramatically, "he offered to bring his business to me, if I decided to open my own consulting shop and bring some of his friends as new clients for me," she ended with a smile.

"Ooh…exciting! Is that what you're going to do? I mean, it sounds like a great idea to me, but where would you work? I mean, when you get up in the morning, where would you drive to?" Jessica asked, curious.

"Well, that's the best part," she said, unable to help herself from breaking into a huge grin, "I could work from home!" she ended, throwing her arms in the air and laughing at the sheer amazement she still felt at the idea. "I'm going to be a small business owner," she ended with pride.

"You're kidding! That's terrific!" Jessica squealed in delight. "I always envied sales people who worked from home, but I never wanted to be in sales," she ended, crinkling her nose. "So, you could live and work anywhere, like right here, in town? From mom's house? Or maybe buy your own house? Jack works with someone whose sister-in-law is a realtor, I think her name is Mary Jane something or other. I'll ask Jack for her number," she continued in a rush, not stopping as she hurriedly grabbed her phone.

"Jessie, wait!" Jillian yelled, laughing at her sister. She was such a marvel when she got going that their dad used to call her Hurricane Jessie when she used to blow through, leaving a trail behind her. "That's the other part of the news," Jillian continued after her sister had settled back into the couch, watching her intently. "I already found a house that I think I want to buy. It's not far from here and it's fabulous! It's a small two bedroom with a really nice yard and great rooms," she continued to describe the house and was thrilled to see Jessica so happy for her. It really was a big step for her, becoming a homeowner - and, possibly a business owner. Her head was spinning, as she realized how much she didn't know anything about either of those two things.

"I already talked to Jack about financing, as a matter of fact, and just have to finish the paperwork."

"Oh Jilly, this will be great! You'll be living back at home, just a few miles away. You'll be your own boss. I'm so excited for you!" she ended, nearly bouncing out of her seat. "This calls for more than just plain, old lemonade," she ran into the kitchen and came back with a bottle of vodka. "Now we can officially celebrate," she declared, adding a healthy shot to both of their glasses. Jillian laughed out loud, relieved that Jessica was just as happy with the prospect as she was.

"So you told me about work, the house, but not about Matt. Is there more good news that you're not telling me?" Jessica asked, taking a long drink of the sweet lemonade they were enjoying.

"There's really nothing to tell. I mean, we've seen each other a few times since I've been back in town. Then we looked at the house the other morning…"

"Wait, what do you mean, 'we looked at the house,'" Jessica asked, zeroing in on the detail that Jillian tried to hurriedly sneak past her. "How did Matt go to look at the house with you? And I don't believe there's nothing to tell. I saw the way Matt was looking at you, so spill the beans," she demanded.

"Come on, Jessica, give me a break. We had a nice dinner, nice conversation, then he dropped me off at home the night of the softball game after you left me stranded at the field. He showed up one morning after I got back from running and finding the house. I had made an appointment with the realtor and he offered to go with me and give me a professional opinion on work that would need to be done. That's it," she ended, hoping Jessica wouldn't pursue the subject. But of course, she did. Her little sister was always so predictable.

"Ok, what else? And don't use the word, nice, please."

Jillian sighed dramatically. She may as well tell Jessica the rest and end the interrogation now or listen to her endless litany of questions for the rest of the afternoon. Not exactly how she wanted to pass the time until her date.

"Well, it's really nothing. But if you must know, Matt called a little while ago and asked me to go to dinner with him tonight," she paused, noticing Jessica's smile. "But it's nothing; just dinner with a friend."

"And a tour of his bed if you're lucky!" Jessica added with a wolfish grin and lewd wink as their mother entered the room.

"A tour of whose bed?" Kate Simmons asked, dropping down onto the couch next to Jessica as Jillian groaned out loud, throwing her arms over her head in a very Scarlet O'Hara pose. Her mother and younger sister laughed at her dramatics. She filled her mother in on the latest happenings and was pleased to see her smile and nod her head encouragingly. She was glad to be back home, she thought, draining the last of her loaded lemonade.

CHAPTER 26

Surveying her limited clothing options and remembering that Matt had said it was a casual dinner, Jillian realized that she didn't have a lot of options. Most of her clothes were still in storage, but there had to be something that would work. After browsing her meager outfits, she settled on a short black sundress that ended a few inches above her knees, with thin spaghetti straps that crisscrossed in the back. The silky material flowed over her curves and accented the golden tan she had been working on since she had a lot of free time. Adding a silver and black necklace that fell just above her cleavage and matching earrings, she slipped into high-heeled black sandals, glad to find this outfit forgotten at the bottom of a suitcase she had grabbed at the storage unit. With her tan, she didn't need a lot of makeup and just added some mascara and lipstick. A last glance in the mirror had her questioning if her outfit was too sexy for the evening, but her mind replayed the scene on the sidewalk with Matt and she smiled to herself as she headed out the door.

The beautiful day was promising to turn into a warm, breezy evening. Throughout the day, she hadn't let her nerves invade her excitement - Jessica and Kate certainly helped with that. After hearing Jessica's final comment about touring Matt's bed, Kate had insisted on hearing the whole story. She was going to tell her mom everything anyway - well mostly everything - but Jessica's colorful comments made the conversation more laughter than words. She hadn't laughed like that in far too long. In fact, she had even laughed at herself for being nervous about tonight.

But now, as she waited for Matt to pick her up, she wondered if she was doing the right thing, having dinner with a man she hadn't seen in years - but one she had quite a history with. It had been a long time since she'd allowed herself to focus on herself as a woman and not Jillian Simmons, Account Executive, as she'd seen herself in the past. It felt good to get dressed up for an evening that wasn't related to a work event and was looking forward to whatever the evening would bring. Glancing at herself in her compact, she freshened her lipstick and dabbed some perfume behind her ears, on her wrists and elbows and a bit behind her knees, where the scent would be the strongest, without being overpowering. When she perspired, which was a given on a warm day like today, the scent would release itself and hopefully be as sweet as when it was first applied. Maybe she was asking for too much, she thought, but didn't have time to consider the thought as Matt knocked on the door.

Though he was wearing black sunglasses, she would've recognized the strong lines of his face anywhere, even behind shades. Offering a smile, he walked through the door she held open for him. He had dressed casually for their date in black pants that expertly fit his long legs and slim hips. A few wisps of dark brown chest hair poked out at the neckline of the polo shirt he was wearing. He walked to where she was standing, his pants rising slightly to reveal that he wasn't wearing socks with the black, leather loafers that looked soft to the touch. Before he reached her, she caught a whiff of the manly scent of his cologne and deeply inhaled, wondering if it smelled as good up close, if she were nibbling on his neck. Her hormones were definitely working overtime, but she enjoyed the sensation she felt go through her body as he greeted her with a firm handshake that lasted a few seconds longer than necessary. His skin was soft to the touch, but she could tell from the texture of his skin that he was a man used to manual labor. She imagined him working in the hot sun, the sweat at his brow and on his back, while the sun deepened his tanned skin. He probably worked without a shirt in the hot summer, his muscles displayed for all to see. She shook her head as she realized he was speaking to her.

"Are you ok?" Matt inquired with a look of concern.

"I'm fine," she replied with a faint smile as she cleared her throat; if he only knew what she had been thinking seconds ago.

With an obvious once-over, he smiled at her and said, "Jillian, you look wonderful." That was an understatement, he thought, eying the short dress that clung to her body in all the right places. Two thin straps held the whispery soft material on her body and he imagined what she would look like out of the dress. When they had dated, she'd been a thin, athletic girl with long limbs and toned muscles. In the years that passed, she had kept her firm muscle tone, while luscious, womanly curves filled out the rest of her body. She was gorgeous, sexy as hell and he wanted to take her no further than his bed and devour her body and soul all night long. But, he reminded himself firmly that it was just a date. That was the past, and they couldn't relive the past, no matter how strong their desire.

It was right, in light of the circumstances. He needed to change the subject and quit staring so deeply into her eyes he thought he would drown in. Think of green pastures, he told himself, using a famous male trick to subside any passionate thoughts that popped up at the wrong time.

"Is Kate home?" he asked, calling her mother by her first name, as he had been doing since their high school days. She said when people called her Mrs. Simmons, she always looked around for her mother-in-law. She much preferred when her daughters' friends called her Kate. It didn't make her feel old.

"No, she's over at Jessica's, babysitting. Jack and Jessica were going to dinner with friends, so the kids have grandma, movies and chocolate sundaes all to look forward to," she ended with a laugh and a shake of her head. "She definitely loves to spoil those two. So, where are we headed?" she asked as he led her out the front door, pulling it shut until the door lock clicked shut.

"I thought we'd drive to the lake and have dinner at a new seafood restaurant that opened a few months ago. I did some of the sub-contracting work for them and know the owners pretty well. Their food is really outstanding. I think you'll like it," he ended, opening the car door for her, enjoying the view as the dress crept up towards the top of her slim, toned thighs. This was going to be a long night, he thought, settling into the driver's seat of the old black mustang he drove when he was off the job. Calling all green pastures, he thought wryly.

"This is a great car, Matt," she said, admiring the leather interior and pristine dashboard.

"Thanks," he said proudly, "I bought it for myself when

my company started showing a profit."

The ride to the lake took over half an hour with traffic heavier in the warm evening. They filled the time with conversation, getting to know one another again. They were oblivious to the other cars on the highway and the beautiful scenery that passed by, too lost in their dialogue. She's so lively, he thought, as she talked about her former job and the people she had worked with. It was easier for her to talk about it all, he realized, since she'd already told him everything that happened. It made him happy that she felt comfortable with him; that she could relax and let her guard down. He hoped she continued to feel that way after he told his story. But, he didn't want to spoil their evening, so he'd wait.

She had a way of talking with her hands when she was trying to describe something or emphasize a point. It was cute, as was the way she looked away during a story, as if she was embarrassed to maintain eye contact. He found himself drawn in and mesmerized by her eyes, which dazzled when she was excited about something. She was like a girl at times, and then at other times quite serious - a bit stubborn - when talking about something she believed in. He found himself becoming deeply attracted to her and wondered what it would be like to kiss her pouty, red lips and run his hands through her silky hair again, while she moaned and squirmed beneath the touch of his hands. He thought of pulling her into his arms right then and there. What would she do, he pondered, if he suggested skipping dinner and spending the evening tangled up together in the sheets.

"Well, here we are," he said, pausing in front of the glass and wooden door. There was a large brass door handle on the door of the seafood restaurant that he grasped with a

160

smile as he ushered her into the restaurant before him.

They had dinner and talked for hours, enjoying one another's company and the delicious food. Each had ordered the sample grilled seafood platter and shared a bottle of sweet, crisp, ice-cold white wine while sitting outside on the deck. It was a gorgeous warm evening with a lovely breeze drifting off of the lake, as boaters enjoyed the warm evening. They laughed and felt comfortable with one another.

"You know, it feels like the past several years never happened. Like we didn't lose touch with one another," Matt said, wiping a bit of melted butter from Jillian's chin with his napkin. It was such a sweet gesture that seemed perfectly natural to both of them, yet she smiled shyly at the intimate moment. He thought he would die if he didn't get to kiss her again and soon.

"I know," Jillian agreed with a sigh of contentment. "I feel the same way, too. I'm having a great time," she added with a smile that he returned until she broke away from his intense gaze. He had a way of looking at someone that wasn't uncomfortable, but made you feel like he was looking straight into your soul. It unnerved her a little because he took a couple of seconds to think about what she said before responding or commenting. He was a great conversationalist and listener.

Neither wanted the evening to end after dinner, so they walked the streets of the lake area, laughing and holding hands. His large and strong, hers small and soft, clasped together while his thumb gently caressed her knuckles. They glanced in the windows of the other restaurants and shops that lined the lake area and found a little club with a country band. The sun had started to go down, yet the evening was still warm.

"Want to go in and listen?" he asked with a nod toward the door. When she smiled her agreement, he gently tugged her hand and led her into the small club. It was dark and the sound of the band spilled out of the back that opened to the lake. They settled into a booth in a far corner of the room. The booth was small and formed a semi-circle around the table so they could sit side-by-side, their arms resting on the table, and watch the musicians. Several patrons were clapping their hands in time with the music, while others simply sat back and enjoyed the leisurely beat of the melodic sounds.

"Have you been here before?" Jillian leaned in close to ask. Her breath was soft and warm on his skin and smelled faintly of wine. He enjoyed the closeness and intimate moment, saying a silent thank you for the small booth they were seated in.

"No," he replied, speaking in her ear. She felt her body tingle from being so physically close to him, smiling as he tapped his fingers to the beat of the music.

She smelled sweet, and he again thought about gently kissing her neck, but the waitress returned with their drinks, momentarily breaking the spell.

Much later, they, along with the rest of the club, were surprised and dismayed when the bartender shouted, "Last call!" knowing the evening was coming to an end. As time had worn on, the music had become livelier and several couples had stood and danced along to the beat. When a slow song started, Matt and Jillian got up and danced next to their table, each marveling at the fit of their two bodies. She was molded perfectly in the curve of his large frame.

His touch was electrifying as he lightly rested his hand on her back. They were so close; she could feel his heartbeat, which quickened as their dance continued. Small caresses, soft breathing, the dimply lit room, the scratchy voice of the singer - it was a perfect moment, one that she knew she would never forget. But just as quickly as it had started, it came to an end as the music stopped. They looked at one another, she slowly opening her eyes and blinking rapidly as she refocused on him, her lips slightly parted as her breathing grew heavier. His head was a few inches from her. When he bent lower, his eyes focused on her lips, she didn't turn away, but gave herself up for the gentle kiss. Feeling no resistance, he deepened the moment and groaned at the sweetness of her lips. He rubbed his hands up and down her back as she wound her hands up and around his neck, running her hands through his hair.

Back at his house, they made their way to his living room and continued the kisses that had started in the restaurant. The long drive back to his house had only heightened the obvious tension in the air. They were both aware of what was next, for they had been at this point before. But this was different; now they were adults, not teenagers. They made their own decisions and were responsible for their own actions – and the consequences of those actions. There would be no one to blame if things went wrong, only themselves.

"Matt," Jillian breathed, as he continued to trail soft kisses along her neck and throat. She was sitting on his lap in the large, overstuffed chair near the French doors that led to the expansive deck he'd built on the back of the house. The door was open, allowing the warm evening breeze to blow through, playing with the hair that escaped her hair tie. Reaching around her neck, Matt pulled her hair free while she gently shook loose the curls, running his hand through the thick tresses.

"Mmm," he sighed, "you're incredible," he said, pausing in his kisses to study her face. With a tentative touch, Matt slowly drew his index finger along the curve of her face. She closed her eyes and enjoyed the touch of his strong, rough hands against her soft skin. It was like rubbing sandpaper on silk, he thought, trailing his finger across her lips where she playfully sucked on it.

"Keep that up," he warned, his voice husky with the passion he was holding back, "and you'll get more than you bargained for," he added, an intense, smoldering look in his eyes that caused a shiver to race down her spine. Some things never change, he thought as he gazed at her sultry expression. The attraction was still there, hidden beneath the years that had separated them. It was just like it had always been.

"Well, you're definitely all grown up," she said teasingly while sneaking a hand inside his shirt, feeling the strong muscles of his chest, causing him to moan. With one hand, she expertly unbuttoned his shirt and twirled her hands through the traces of brown chest hair. Her touch was light as she barely touched his skin, but she could still feel the heat radiating from his tense body. Without breaking eye contact, she continued rubbing her hand on his hot skin as she leaned in, touching her lips to his in a slow, gentle kiss that seemed to last a lifetime. Not in a hurry to get anywhere other than where they were at the moment, they lingered and enjoyed themselves. He drew her closer to him so that her chest was pressed against his. Her arms moved around his neck to play with the strands of hair curling at his neck. Shifting slightly on his lap, her dress crept up considerably as he continued to rub the tight, firm muscles of her tanned things, enjoying the feel of her soft, velvety skin under his hands. They both had flashbacks to the many hot nights they'd shared in the backseat of his car, getting to know each other's bodies with all of the excitement and anxiousness of teenagers. Back then there had also been the fear that they'd take things too far, not ready for that next step. Neither had wanted to do something that had consequences they could have regretted. This was different and they both knew it. He knew he should stop this now, but he couldn't break away from Jillian. There was something about her that had him coming back for more.

He wanted more of her, more from her, yet he knew he couldn't do that. No matter how much he tried to reason with himself, her lips, her body, her sweetness where all too intoxicating and he felt himself crossing the line of no return; but he didn't care. Leaning forward, he easily stood up with her in his arms, their lips never parting. She felt like a feather in his arms, one that he didn't want to see blow away, yet he couldn't ask her to stay. Not now, things were too complicated. Pulling away from her, he stopped in his tracks and stared at her for a long moment. He had to stop this. There was no doubt he wanted to take her to bed right now, but he knew he couldn't do that.

"Jillian," he breathed, as the phone began to ring.

"Don't answer it," she murmured, her voice husky, her lips raw, as the phone rang again.

"Maybe I should," he started to say and then stopped as he heard his own voice reciting the recorded message.

"You still have an answering machine?" she laughed, looking at him with a gleam in her eyes as he shifted her in his lap, not sure what to do as the beep on the machine let the caller leave their message.

"It's just for business," he murmured as a bad feeling had settled in his stomach. Before the caller had started to speak, he knew that he should have picked up the phone.

"Hey darling," a female voice began, sounding more like a purr, her voice sugary sweet, "guess you're not there. I'm home and wanted to come over for a late-night visit, but I'll guess we'll just have to wait until tomorrow for that. Call me," she whispered before hanging up.

Jillian felt as if time had stopped. She didn't know what to do or say. The room was completely silent and still as neither one of them breathed a word. She didn't know what to say. The only sounds were the chirps from the insects of the night, whose melodious songs were carried on the breeze blowing through the open door. Her entire body had gone rigid when the caller started speaking into the answering machine. Even before the entire message was spoken, she knew it wasn't Matt's sister calling; that was clear from the first whispered words. It had been more intimate and personal than a call from a sister to a brother. It was more like a lover. She felt like someone had slapped her in the face. The ringing in her ears was so loud; it was like a marching band was parading through the room at full volume. She didn't know what to say, what to think, but she did know she felt like a fool.

Without a word, she separated herself from Matt, sliding to her feet and standing directly in front of him, a few feet apart. Much farther apart that they were a few seconds ago. She looked up at him and saw that he was unable to return her gaze. His hands were clenched in tight fists at his side as though he was ready for a fight. There was nothing to fight about. He had a girlfriend. Obviously,

Jillian was just a way to pass the time while she wasn't home. She shouldn't be so upset and angry, but she was, mostly in light of recent events in her life.

"Jillian," Matt whispered, his voice ragged, finally looking up to meet her eyes. "I'm sorry, I don't," he started, but she cut him off.

"That's ok, Matt," she said in a voice that was stronger than she felt. "I get it now. This was going to be a one-night stand while your girlfriend wasn't home. I mean, we were just two old friends catching up. It wasn't going to mean anything," she finished lamely, feeling her throat tighten. She'd been such a fool! Here she was, with her high school boyfriend, making out like a teenager, when all this time he was seeing someone else. Now she knew what it felt like to be the "other woman," and she didn't like it one bit. It made her feel cheap and worthless, as if he could just discard her when he had tired of her and move to whatever was next. Looking at him and knowing what she'd heard, it was still hard to believe this was happening with Matt. He'd always been so honest and loving. She couldn't believe he'd done this to her. But time had a way of changing people, she mused.

"You're right," he said, defeated as he stood with his hands on his hips, shaking his head, "I should have told you about Kimberly. I was going to, then the phone rang and well," he trailed off, not sure what else to say. There was nothing he could say that would make her feel less foolish. She wasn't sure that she could get her body to move. Her feet felt like lead, but she knew she had to get out of his house.

"It's ok...like I said before, it's no big deal," she said, getting a little angrier at hearing his girlfriend's name. She thought for a minute that maybe she'd jumped to conclusions, but his saying her name made it a reality. Right now, she just wanted to leave, crawl into her bed and forget this evening had ever happened. What was it about her that made men cheat and betray her? First Kevin, now Matt? In retrospect, the first one didn't surprise her. Kevin had been a snake and she should've seen that, but she'd been blinded by his charm, charisma and money to see him for what he really was. But Matt did surprise her, and that made her angry. They'd been going out - granted it was casual - but it had been nearly a month, and he hadn't said a word. What was wrong with her?!

"No, Jillian," he said angrily, grabbing her upper arms tightly, "it doesn't matter. You don't understand. I didn't want to just spend the night with you, I wanted to…"

"What Matt? What did you want to do?" she nearly shouted at him, shocking both of them with the anger that had crept into her voice. Pulling away from him, she raced around for her purse and shoes. She had to get out of his house - away from him. She was such a fool! "Why didn't you tell me you were seeing someone? It would have saved me the embarrassment of finding out like this! I've got to get out of here," she said, shoving her shoes on her feet as she marched to the front door with him racing after her. She was breathless, her heart threatening to beat right out of her chest.

"Jillian, wait," he said, catching her by the waist and turning her around to face him. "Let me explain. You can't just walk out and not give me a chance to explain."

"Oh, yes I can, and that's exactly what I'm doing!" she responded, wriggling free of his grasp before opening the door and walking out into the night. "I had a nice evening, until a few minutes ago. You should have told me, Matt. Damn it! You're just like Kevin. Please don't call me. Message received." She turned and walked down the sidewalk in the direction of her mother's house without a backward glance. The tears started the moment she stepped outside. Earlier, the air had seemed light and refreshing, but now it threatened to choke her if she didn't get away from his house. Tears blinded her eyes and she ran on. Slowing down as she saw the front door, she tried to even her ragged breath, wiping the tears from her face. It looked as though her mother wasn't home yet, and she was grateful. She changed her clothes, wiped off her makeup and crawled in bed, knowing sleep wouldn't come easily tonight. The night insects continued singing their song well after the moon shifted across the sky and the hours ticked by.

CHAPTER 27

Matt couldn't believe what happened. Damn it! He knew Jillian had a right to be angry, but seeing her fury and unwillingness to listen to him surprised him. He was wrong. He knew that. He should have told her about Kimberly, but what was he supposed to say. "Oh, by the way, I'm planning on breaking up with my girlfriend, but haven't found the right time to do it." That's not exactly the way to a girl's heart. But it would probably have been better for her than hearing Kimberly leave such an intimate message on his answering machine as they were seconds away from heading to his bed.

In his mind, he and Kim had already gone through the break-up woes and tears that women indulge in when a relationship ends, but of course that wasn't true. Kimberly was as much in his life today as she was when they'd first started dating. He'd been remodeling her house, found her attractive and asked her out to dinner. It was as simple as that, and they'd been dating off and on for the past six months. But he was ready for it to be off for good. It wasn't that he didn't enjoy her company. She was certainly good company, in and out of bed, more than willing to share her body with him. But that was all they had. They really didn't have anything in common other than the physical activities. That would be enough for some men, and it had been for him, but seeing Jillian again changed that. Like most men, he liked sports and enjoyed sitting back at home on a Sunday afternoon with a cold beer and an afternoon of armchair quarterbacking. Kim couldn't stand football, or any sports for that matter. He liked classic rock and country, while she preferred classical music. He liked watching movies, she didn't. In fact, he thought, what had made him ask her out in the first place? But, he knew it was a numbers answer…36-28-36, blonde and blue.

He knew he should've grabbed the phone before the old machine picked up, but he forgot it was even there most times, using his cell as his main phone. The answering machine was for his older customers who didn't understand leaving a message on a cell phone was the same as an answering machine. She must have called his cell, and not getting an answer, had tried the old landline. He was going to have to call her and break it off in person. He owed her that; he couldn't just dump her. She would be too hurt, and he wasn't the kind of guy to intentionally hurt someone.

CHAPTER 28

First thing Monday morning, Jillian called Mary Jane, the realtor and asked if she could see the house again. She wanted her mom and Jessie to see it before she made a final decision. Mary Jane agreed to meet them at the house in an hour. Jillian's mind soared at the thought of being a homeowner. It was what she needed at this time in her life and she was ready for the responsibility. It was time to make some decisions about her life and move forward, not back.

After a disastrous ending to the wonderful evening she and Matt had, she was awake most of the night thinking about her plans and what she wanted to do with her future. She cried and then chastised herself for crying, but eventually the tears stopped and she fell asleep for a few hours. It was easy to think about what others should do, but she'd always found it hard to decide what she wanted to do for herself. It was like she was always waiting for someone else to make her decisions for her. Someone else to draw the roadmap of her future, pushing her in the right direction so she did what she was supposed to do, what was right for her, not everyone else. That had gotten her hurt in the past and she needed to change her way of thinking. She had to worry about Jillian and what she wanted for herself,

172

not what anyone else wanted or thought she should do. Focus on what she wanted to do and how to make it happen.

It was all very exciting, she thought, as her mom and Jessie walked around the house. With her eyes closed, she could picture how the house was going to look furnished with her style stamped everywhere. Nothing would be stark or sterile, as it was in Kevin's house. Actually, Matt's house was more along the lines of how she would decorate a house. His home had a simpler, homey and comfortable style. But after what happened last night, she needed to push him out of her mind. Sure, they'd been close to crossing that invisible line that defined the difference between good, old friends and lovers. They were two people attracted to one another with a lot in common, but he was seeing someone and hadn't told her. She still liked him a lot, but after last night, she knew he wasn't going to be part of her future as a friend or a contractor. Glancing around, she thought of the ideas he had about redesigning the house that she would still incorporate, but with another contractor.

"Oh honey, it's just perfect," Kate enthused, coming out of the kitchen. "The kitchen is lovely and you have a lot of room for entertaining. I do see what you mean about some of the work that needs done, but I'm sure Matt can handle that for you without a problem."

"Well," she began, not wanting to get into a discussion about Matt. She wasn't going to tell either of them about last night. It was personal, embarrassing and not something she wanted to share and this wasn't the time or place anyway.

"He's pretty busy, so I don't think I'm going to worry

about any major remodeling right now. Besides, there's nothing so critical that I can't move in immediately. It's not like the roof is falling in or the furnace doesn't work. I can add a fresh coat of paint to the walls myself, if I want" she finished, not quite meeting their eyes. She hated not being able to confide in her mother or sister, but embarrassment and hurt ran deep.

"Jilly, Jack and I can help you paint," Jessica offered, putting an arm around her sister's waist and planting a noisy kiss on her cheek.

"Me, too," Kate called, joining her daughters in the impromptu hug in the middle of the living room floor. They broke out in a chorus of giggles, hugging one another, each thrilled that Jillian was coming home to stay. The laughter was just what Jillian needed to focus her mind on.

"I'll take it!" she called over her shoulder to Mary Jane, who was smiling at the trio of women.

Mary Jane took her phone out of her purse, "Let me call the executor of the estate and discuss the details. Give me fifteen minutes," she smiled, walking into the kitchen to make the call in privacy.

"Wow," Jillian breathed, looking around her with wide eyes. "I can't believe I'm buying a house!" She was amazed at how funny life was sometimes. A few weeks ago, she was living in the city - now she was buying a house back in her hometown. If someone had told her that then, she'd have called them crazy.

The realtor walked back into the living room where the three women had settled on the floor. "I have very good news, Jillian," she began with a smile. "The estate is willing to accept your offer, which is about $5,000 below the asking price, but they're happy to get it sold and close the estate," she explained. "So, we just need to take care of the financing on your end and sign the papers. Give me a call when you're ready to meet this week and finalize, but I think I can say with some confidence that you'll be able to move in before the end of the month," she concluded with a smile and a handshake for Jillian who had bounced up from her spot on the floor.

A thousand thoughts ran through her head. She had to choose paint colors, replace some of the fixtures in the upstairs bathroom, arrange to move her furniture from the storage facility in the city. It was going to be so much fun! She was looking forward to browsing through the thrift stores around town for some interesting trinkets and decorations. She knew her mom and Jessie would be more than happy to join her on those expeditions. She couldn't wait to be a homeowner and have something to look forward to that didn't involve the men who insisted on making her life complicated. At that moment, she didn't care about Kevin's betrayal, losing her job or Matt and his girlfriend. She was going to be a homeowner and a businesswoman - and she was doing it all on her own.

CHAPTER 29

Life had been moving quickly the past couple of weeks. Jillian had bid on the house, was approved for her mortgage and was working the application for her small business loan with the help of Jack, her banking brother-in-law. She completed the state required business organization forms, fictitious name paperwork and countless other forms that she was able to file online.

With all of that, she'd made arrangements to move her belongings home and booked her travel to Texas to meet with Rick Colbert. Before she met with him, Jillian had to take time to prepare to represent herself as a business owner, not an employee of someone else's company.

Jillian was feeling pleased with everything she'd accomplished. Maybe this will be a season of change for her, she thought, a time to finally take charge of what she wanted.

When she woke up not feeling well, she figured she was exhausted and mentally drained. But as the morning wore on, she started feeling a little nauseous. Maybe she was getting a bug. Even though it was summer, she knew getting sick was a possibility. Well, she had been running non-stop morning to night, from gathering her financial records the bank needed to meeting with Jack to complete the paperwork to selecting paint colors and everything she needed for the house to setting up her own business. There was a lot of detail and work involved with that venture, especially since it was such a risk. She knew how to do her job, but she didn't know anything about running a company, but she did know how to work with people, see their vision and help them make it happen. That's what she was getting into now, feeling her confidence swell she she'd been doing that for a few years. There wouldn't be a learning curve like there was when you started a new job. The hard part was the paperwork required by the state and IRS, choosing her own health care and insurance to purchase, setting up her home office and becoming profitable. She'd been reviewing her business plan when exhaustion got the best of her. She headed back to the family room to close her eyes for a bit.

"Jillian, wake up," Kate whispered, gently shaking her oldest daughter's shoulder. She'd come home from work and found Jillian curled up on the couch under a small blanket and was worried about her. Jillian had been running herself ragged lately, and Kate hoped she hadn't worn herself to the point of exhaustion.

"Huh..." Jillian murmured, slowly opening her eyes and trying to get a grasp of her surroundings, "What time is it?" she croaked, her throat dry from sleeping. She was disoriented and unsure where she was. Raising a trembling hand to her forehead, she was startled to find her hands so clammy and her face so warm. It must be from the blanket she was wrapped under.

"It's 4:30 in the afternoon. I just got home from work and found you here sleeping. Aren't you feeling well?" Kate asked, laying a concerned hand on her daughter's forehead to check for a fever. "You do feel a little warm, but maybe you're just tired. You've been so busy lately, trying to get everything done that you probably just wore yourself out."

"Yeah, you're right. I came in here to lay down, but I didn't think I'd fall asleep for so long," Jillian said taking her time getting to her feet. Feeling a little dizzy, she sat back down and rested her head in her hands, taking her fingers through her hair.

"I think everything going on has finally settled in on you," Kate whispered as she added a soft kiss to Jillian's head. "How about you freshen up and we go out to dinner? Get out and get some fresh air. Slow down for a bit and relax."

CHAPTER 30

After ordering, Jillian and Kate sat back and relaxed in the comfortable booth, enjoying the peaceful atmosphere and outdoor seating of the diner. When it had first opened in the late 60's, the diner had been a small one-room building, with enough tables for about 30 people and a counter where patrons could sit on barstools and eat while watching their food being prepared on the grill behind the counter. Barren in terms of decorations and atmosphere, the diner kept a thriving business of regular customers with the good, home cooked and reasonably priced meals they served.

The waitresses wore the standard uniforms of that day, resembling those favored by the old TV show, Alice. It was a family-owned business that had been handed down through the generations, along with the recipe for their famous chili. Nobody had ever come close to repeating the dish at home and those who cooked it in the restaurant wouldn't reveal the secret ingredients.

As the years passed, the diner continued to serve the same good food they always had, while growing and expanding. They added a back deck where small patio tables with umbrellas and booths were always grabbed first when the weather was nice. There was the new back room that could be rented for group events and parties. But will all of the new changes, there were some things that hadn't changed. The charm and atmosphere were the same. The waitress's uniforms were updated to black shorts and a white t-shirt with the diner's name and logo on the back. However, they still put their customers' happiness and satisfaction first.

Sighing deeply and glancing around her, Jillian took in her surroundings, relaxing for the first time in days. "This is nice," she smiled, enjoying the light breeze and warmth of the sun, feeling better than she had earlier in the day.

"You've been working so hard lately. I hope you haven't worn yourself out. Take a few days off and just relax," Kate suggested, reaching across the table to squeeze her daughter's hand. "You've always been such a hard worker, trying to do everything all at once, not taking the time to catch your breath and enjoy the moment. I don't want to see you making yourself sick," she added with a worried smile.

"Mom, don't worry about me. I mean, I know you worry and it's your job as a mother, but I'm doing fine. I finally feel like I'm in control of my life. I'm 29 years old and am buying my first house, opening a business where I can be my own boss and I already have a client waiting to pay me to work for him. I'm going to be fine." Even though she was addressing the remarks to her mother, she was also saying them to herself. She was going to ok and the sooner she started to believe that, the better off she'd be. She knew that, but was more critical of herself than anyone.

"So, tell me about your date with Matt. Is there something going on there?" Kate had always been fond of Matt. He was polite, intelligent, good looking and from a good family, though he and his sister lost their parents shortly after he'd graduated from college. She'd been disappointed when Jillian and Matt had broken-up, but her daughter's happiness came first, though she thought Matt made her happy.

"It wasn't really a date, mom, we just had dinner and listened to some music," she downplayed it, not wanting to discuss Matt or the sour note their evening ended on. "Besides, he's dating someone and is busy with his own business. And we're just friends, so there's really nothing to tell."

That was enough. She didn't need to say anything else or her mom would detect just how upset she really was, deep down inside. Her head and mind had gotten carried away on a tangent where she pictured them dating, falling in love and picking up in their relationship where they'd left off. Now she knew better and admonished herself for acting like a ridiculous schoolgirl.

Looking at her mother, she turned her head to see what had caught Kate's attention on the other side of the deck. She couldn't believe her eyes. This was impossible, she thought angrily. Of all the restaurants in the area, they showed up at the same one, on the same evening at the same time. It was unbelievable, and she found that she'd lost her appetite. She watched him hold out a chair from the table for the slim, petite blonde at a table for two. Jillian watched in disbelief as Matt helped someone into her seat. She tried not to notice how good he looked, but tried to focus her attention on his dinner partner. From the pictures, she'd seen at his house, she knew this blonde wasn't his sister, so she had to be Kimberly, the faceless caller who'd called during their romantic encounter. Matt's eyes locked on her, as she quickly turned around, hoping he hadn't recognized her, which was silly. She closed her eyes and wished the floor would open up and swallow her whole. They hadn't even gotten their dinners and she was ready to leave.

"Honey, isn't that Matt?" Kate wondered out loud as she raised her hand to wave, suddenly adding a smile to her face that expressed her confusion, "Well, hello there, nice to see you."

"Good evening, Kate," Matt smiled warmly, reaching down to hug his former girlfriend's mom, while glancing at Jillian.

Awkward didn't begin to describe the setting. It wasn't impossible for him to read the expression on Jillian's face. She was trying her best to paint on a smile, but it wasn't working. He could see the agitation bubbling just beneath the surface as she remained silent.

"Well, it was nice seeing you. I better get back," he said, then turned on his heel and headed back to his table. Why did he let her get to him like that?

"Nice seeing you, Matt," Kate called as he departed. "You could have been a little politer, Jillian. Regardless of what happened or didn't happen between you two, I didn't raise my daughters to forget their social graces and manners," she reprimanded.

Despite all of her attempts to salvage the evening, Jillian couldn't shoo Matt from her mind. She enjoyed the dinner with her mother as best she could, but her thoughts weren't with the conversation she and Kate were having. She wished she could get him out of her head, but no matter how hard she tried, she still pictured him that evening with the sultry, sexy look in his eyes. But, he'd lied to her and betrayed her. Those were things she couldn't forget.

She still wasn't feeling great and seeing Matt with the blonde bombshell hadn't helped. Her head was throbbing and she just wanted to go home and hide under the covers until the headache cleared.

Just one more disaster to add the list, she thought giving into the self-pity she thought she had pushed away. Buying a house, starting your own business and becoming independent for the first time in a long time didn't do anything for her mood now. She wanted to wallow in her sudden depression again.

CHAPTER 31

"Matt, who was that?" Kimberly asked in her squeaky voice that he'd once found amusing, but recently started to annoy him. He almost felt bad for her because that was the kind of person he was. His mother had always called him her 'sensitive son.' He missed his parents. The ache of losing the people who gave you life, raised you and molded you into the person you eventually became was something you didn't recover from easily. He and his sister had been close to their parents and their passing had come with years of heartache and grief.

"Just some old friends. What do you want to drink? Let's order." Because there are a few things we need to talk about, Matt added to himself, not liking the direction the conversation was going to take. But even if Jillian wasn't going to be part of his life, he knew Kimberly had to go. She'd become too clingy, calling him constantly wanting to know what he was doing. She'd even gone so far as to visit him on a construction site, eliciting whistles and hot glances from his workers until they realized she was there to see him. She'd make up flimsy excuses about something that needed fixed at her house, but it was just an excuse to stop by and see him. He'd put an end to that after the third time telling her that he wouldn't tolerate her interruptions at work and that a construction site wasn't safe for her to just drop in. Her visits were far too dangerous. They caused his crew to lose their concentration. One wrong move and someone could cut off a finger, fall off of a roof or seriously hurt someone else. Not only that, she didn't have any business being there. After that explanation and the tears she'd work up, she'd heeded his warning and hadn't returned. But the phone calls had continued. Kimberly would call at all hours of the day and night when she wasn't next to him in bed. In the beginning, it was cute, but now it was just too much. He used to like when she'd spend the night, but now he wanted to untangle himself from her, especially because of Jillian. Kimberly wasn't taking the hints he threw at her - like when he said he was tired and just wanted to go to bed, and she should sleep at her own house. She needed to move on and find someone else. She was a nice woman, but she wasn't Jillian. It hadn't taken him long to realize that once Jillian had slammed back into his life. That wasn't something he ever thought possible, but here he was.

He knew it wasn't going to be easy. If there was one thing Kimberly loved, it was a good fight followed by even better make-up sex. He was hoping ending their relationship in a public place, like the diner where they were having dinner would eliminate that drama.

Nope. He was wrong. She'd thrown a tantrum in the middle of the back deck, crying the entire time, telling him she'd change, she'd be whatever he wanted her to be. It was embarrassing and he cursed himself for not knowing better. He should have just stopped over her house after work and had the discussion, not try to have a friendly breakup in a public place. He didn't understand women and didn't think he ever would. She should have been more humiliated than he was since she was the one who had caused the scene. But she'd probably get sympathy from her friends because of the way he'd ended their relationship, claiming that she had no idea why he was being so mean to her. She wouldn't see if for what it was.

Relationships started, some continued and grew into long-term commitments while others that were never meant to be from the start just ended. That's just the way it was. He hadn't made up the rules; he was just trying to survive the game.

Then, on top of Kimberly's academy award winning antics, Jillian had acted as though he didn't exist. She wouldn't even look at him and her greeting was as cold and frosty as an arctic blast. That was another woman he couldn't understand. She'd been so sweet, charming and fun on their date, that he wasn't completely sure she was the same person he'd seen tonight. Her mother had been. Then again, Kate had always been fond of him. It's Jillian's fault he hadn't been able to tell her about Kimberly, he reasoned. She'd run out before he had a chance to explain.

He was going to forget about women, he decided, and focus his energy elsewhere. He'd managed to remove Kimberly from his life and it was obvious Jillian didn't want to be part of his life. Frustrated, he changed into running clothes and headed out the front door as the sun was just starting to set. Maybe a twilight run would help work off some of his anger, if not his confusion.

CHAPTER 32

Even though the closing on her house was still a few weeks away, the estate representatives had given Jillian a key and told her she could begin whatever work she wanted to do. The waiting was just a technicality, just some red tape since she already submitted her accepted offer. She appreciated the gesture and didn't waste time on the work she wanted to do before moving in.

With that in mind, she first headed over with buckets, bottles of cleaning products, a bag of rags, a broom and a mop. Jessica had volunteered her time and had shown up with a couple bottles of wine coolers. Together they wiped down all the walls, dusting away the cobwebs and dirt that had settled during the many months the house sat unoccupied. Turning up the radio, they sang along with the classic hits from the 80's and 90's that had been their jam back in the day.

"Oh Matt, you're so fine, you're so fine you blow my mind, hey Matty," Jessie sang along substituting the lyrics of Mickey with Matt, hoping to get a laugh out of her sister.

"Ha ha, very funny Jess…" Jillian smiled.

They swept and mopped the floors, used the rented steam cleaner on the rugs both upstairs and downstairs. It was looking good and began to resemble a comfortable living space again. Now that it had been deep cleaned, she was ready to paint.

That had been the fun part. Jillian loved visiting home stores and digging into paint samples and wallpaper swatches, trying to envision the colors she'd use throughout the house. She could see herself sipping her morning coffee in the living room and cooking dinners for... She'd been thinking of Matt, she realized, but he wouldn't be eating dinner at her house. He'd be eating his dinners with Kimberly, his girlfriend. It was startling to her that he invaded her thoughts so quickly and naturally. Sometimes he'd just pop in her head without any warning. Her feelings for Matt had really started to develop again. Spending time with him was a true joy. Shaking her head, she reminded herself that he wasn't hers. Moving on, that's what she had to do, again. After finishing a cooler, she turned to the next chore and got busy.

A few days later she was armed with cans of paint, rollers and tape spread out on the drop cloths. Now she could see the house coming together. It already had a sense of home to her as she slowly started rolling the paint on the living room walls. It felt incredible!

She was lost in her thoughts, singing along to the radio she'd brought over from her mom's house to keep her company, but the sound of gravel crunching under tires in her driveway brought her out of her reverie. It was probably her mom bringing over some dinner, she thought, wiping the paint from her hands. She said she might stop over after Jessica picked her kids up.

But, the footsteps that fell on her porch were much heavier than Kate's and she was startled and let out a gasp when the face of her visitor was visible through the screen door. He was the last person she expected to find on her doorstep. Well, wasn't this going to be interesting, she thought with a wry shake of her head.

"Can I come in?" Kevin asked when she answered the door.

"Well, this is a surprise. What are you doing here? I can't imagine what there is to say. I thought we settled everything there was between us last time we saw one another. I mean, your email definitely hit home for me that it's over."

"Jillian, I'm sorry. I was such a fool to let things get so out of hand. I should have told you everything before. It didn't have to end the way it did," Kevin paused to take a deep breath, "Actually, it didn't have to end at all."

"Oh no, that's where you're wrong," she said flatly, "you betrayed me, lied to me, kept secrets from me and those are things I can't forgive." She turned away so he couldn't see how emotional she'd become. Of all people, she couldn't let herself breakdown in front of him. "You know," she started again, turning around slowly to face him, "It's taken me time to get over this. I cried a lot of tears, but that's in the past and I'm moving forward. I don't need you in my life, nor do I want you."

With a heavy sigh, he ran his hand through his hair and looked at her sternly. "Well, this isn't exactly the warm reception I expected. I can't believe you're going to stand there and be this callous and hard. What happened to the

Jillian I used to know? The sweet, forgiving girl I fell in love with?"

"You know what, Kevin, she got hurt one time too many by you," she replied firmly. "There's nothing to discuss. You betrayed me and I learned a valuable lesson from the whole experience. Now, if you'll excuse me, I don't know how you found me, and I have painting to do. I don't need you, your help and I don't want you in my new house. And how did you find me anyway? Nobody knows this address," she exclaimed, then glanced at her phone.

"Are you tracking my phone? Seriously? Kevin! I'm no longer your concern! Delete my number from your phone now or I'll do it for you! I can't believe you've been tracking me! You chose Alexis and the company, left me without a job or a home, and you're still keeping an eye on me? Give me a break and get out of my house!"

With that, she waited until he walked back to his car. When he turned around and started talking to her, she quietly and firmly closed the door, putting that chapter of her life to rest.

Unable to settle down, Jillian plopped down on the floor and cracked open a wine cooler from the fridge. She couldn't believe Kevin tracked her down! Hearing a car door slam outside, she jumped up, huffing, ready to scream at him if he didn't leave her the hell alone!

"Kevin!" she yelled directly into Jessica's face that was peering at her through the open door.

"Whoa! What's your problem? Are you ok?" Jessica asked, frightened by her older sister's unexpected fury.

"Oh my god, Jessie! I thought you were Kevin."

"Um, why would I be Kevin?" Jessica asked as she eased into the house, taking in her sister's agitated demeanor, as she dropped her purse on the floor.

"He was just here and I pretty much threw him out of the house!" Jillian yelled, sliding to the floor and putting her head in her hands with a groan.

"Why would you invite Kevin HERE?"

"Jessie, he was tracking my phone. I didn't invite him over. I haven't talked to him and didn't plan on talking to him ever again," she said with a sob, letting the whole story out.

"That's crazy, just crazy. I mean, he's been stalking you? Like on a Dateline episode or something?" Jessie finished with a deep sip of her drink and smack of her lips.

"Cheers to no more stalking," she said, clinking her cup with Jillian's can.

"For sure! Hey, what are you guzzling in that Yeti?" Jillian asked, eyeing the drink Jessica had just finished.

"Oh, it's just my mommy's little sippy cup," Jessica shrugged, and stashed the mug in her purse, evading Jillian's inquiring eyes.

"What does that mean? Is it alcohol? Did you drive over here drinking? Jess…what is going on with you? First all the wine when we had lasagna dinner, then the vodka lemonade and now this? What is going on that's making you drink so much?"

"Hold on a minute, Jillian, we're talking about you and your life. Not mine."

"I've been meaning to ask you about this anyway, this drinking of yours. I'm worried about you. What are you doing?"

"You listen to me, big sister," Jessica jumped up, raising her voice as she stalked around the room waving her arms, surprising both sisters with the sudden anger in her voice. "Not everyone gets to be Saint Jillian! I don't have to explain myself to you. So, I have a few drinks every now and then; so what? It's not a big deal and I have it under control."

"Under control? What's that supposed to me? How is your life out of control? My life is in tatters, in case you've forgotten," Jillian said in a raised tone of voice, waving her arms around. "I'm the one who was very recently homeless and unemployed. Two things I didn't exactly plan for!"

"Well, I'm sorry for you. Once again, everything is about Saint Jillian! Not everyone got to leave home, go to college and come home for a day or two at a time with everyone rolling out the red carpet! Mom used to clean for days before Jillian was deigning us commoners with a visit! You know how much she worried about if Jillian would want chicken or beef stew to eat, did we have new bath towels so Saint Jillian wouldn't have to use old ratty towels after her shower, did we have the coffee creamer you liked or the right kind of pop because Jillian liked Coke and not Pepsi," Jessica's voice cracked as she started to cry.

"Don't tell me about anything or about what I'm drinking.

You don't know what it was like to get through life with mom in the years after you left for college, when mom walked around the house lost, missing dad after he passed away. There were nights she wouldn't sleep for more than half an hour, but always added some energy to her voice when you called because we couldn't let Jillian know how rough things were. I had to get a job at the bank to help her pay the bills! I couldn't run away to college and put my family out of my mind and just worry about myself. Oh no, not me, not Jessica. We had to make sure Jillian didn't know so she could concentrate on college and finishing her degree!"

"What are you talking about?" Jillian asked with a start. "You think I was off having a great time? I was in college, working my ass off waitressing on the side so I could pay the bills my scholarship didn't cover. I wasn't exactly bar hopping and going to frat every night!"

"Oh, don't give me that shit, you know you couldn't wait to get out of the house and be the big shot who left town and was off making something of herself. I couldn't leave, I couldn't leave mom alone, so my dreams were squashed when I went to work at the bank. Then I met Jack, got married and pregnant and that was the end of my career!

Jillian's eyes were huge at this announcement. "What are you talking about? You have everything! You have a husband who treats you like a princess, two amazing kids and you don't have to worry about your next paycheck not coming. I don't have any of that! None, not one piece. You have it all! You're the one with everything and I'm struggling to put my life back together!"

Both sisters suddenly ran out of steam, tears streaming down their cheeks, out of breath at the rush of words and accusations flying around. They never fight; not like this. This was new and different and didn't feel good to either one.

"Ugh...." Jessica said with a start, realizing she had divulged a very big secret she'd kept from her sister for all those years. This was not how she wanted it to happen, in a near-drunken stupor and in a heated moment.

"Come here..." Jillian whispered, pulling Jessica down on the floor next to her, rubbing her hair as she sobbed. "It's ok... Everything is ok. I had no idea, Jessie. Why didn't you tell me? What happened? I didn't know about mom. She was always so upbeat when I called and didn't share anything like what you just said."

"She didn't want you to know," Jessica murmured into her sister's hair as she tried to catch her breath. "She used to make sure she was dressed and put together for when you would call or visit; she didn't want you to know how much pain she was really in. It was so hard on all of us, but you left. You got to leave. You didn't have to walk through the rooms dad walked through or look at his empty seat at the table. Remember the old kitchen table? One day I made mom get a new table and chair set because I couldn't look at his empty chair anymore," she sighed, wiping her eyes.

CHAPTER 33

After dinner that evening, Jillian found Kate settled in front of the TV to stream the latest episode of Blue Bloods. All three Simmons ladies love the show and traded texts throughout as the Reagan family kept New York safe and shared a family meal each Sunday. Maybe we can start a Simmons Sunday family dinner tradition when I get settled, Jillian thought, picturing everyone crowded around the dining room table in her new house.

"Mom, can we talk for a minute?

"Sure sweetie," Kate said, pausing the show and turning towards Jillian on the couch.

"Why didn't you tell me how tight things were after dad died, when I went to college? I could have helped."

"What do you mean, honey? We were fine. Your sister and I were fine."

"Well, not according to Jessica. She tore into me at the new house the other evening when I was painting. She told me she had to get a job to help pay the bills at home. She basically blamed me for her not getting to go to college. I mean, I didn't have a clue what was happening with my own family," she said as a small sob escaped her.

"Oh Jillian, we were fine. The house was fine," Kate said patting Jillian's hand.

"Not according to Jessie. She made it sound like you were in jeopardy of losing the house. She even called me Saint Jillian!"

"Oh my," Kate chuckled, "She must have been in a mood! But, joking aside, I mean, it was tough. I was sad, I'm still sad. I missed your dad - the life we built and the plans we'd made, so it probably took me longer to get back on my feet. You can't place a time limit on grieving. I did the best I could, and so did your sister."

"I feel bad that I'm just finding out when I could have done something to help."

"Jillian, my baby," Kate cooed into her hair as she wrapped her arms around her oldest daughter, "if I had told you or your sister had told you, what would you have done?"

"I'd have dropped out and come home to help out!"

"Exactly why I insisted we didn't tell you. College was the right fit for you. You needed to get out of your hometown and start down your own path, your own dreams. Your sister wasn't ready to move out of the house after she graduated. You're different people, my two J girls. You were happy in school and doing great. Your sister needed a little more time at home and it fit the situation. Then she met Jack, fell in love and everything fell into place for her. Did she help me out with finances? Yes, she definitely did, until I was ready to get out and back into the job market. I can't ever say it was fair, but it's what we did and it worked for us. She got a job when she was ready and I did the same. You may forget that daddy's life insurance paid off most of the major expenses we had, so we weren't ever in jeopardy of losing the house. I wouldn't have let that happen. Your father and I made our life in this house and that's not something you throw away. You'll see when you start to get settled in your house that everything you do to it becomes part of you and you do whatever you can to protect it. Plus, your sister needed me a bit more than you did, so it gave us the time we all needed."

"Thanks for being so open and honest, mom. I feel bad and worry now that I know what happened, that I could have done more."

"Jillian, we all did what we needed to do, and were healing in our own ways."

After talking to her mom, Jillian needed to get outside to get some fresh air and clear her head. The fight with Jessica still weighed heavy on her. She didn't realize her sister had been dealing with so much over the past few years. Maybe she was naïve or maybe she intentionally missed the signs that things at home weren't as great as she thought. They kept so much from her so that she could focus on moving forward. She'd revisit things with Jessica and keep a closer eye on her drinking, whether her sister liked it or not, now that she was home.

And now hearing things from her mom's perspective, she realizes she did miss out on a lot, but she wasn't to blame like Jessica thought. She wondered if Jessica's drinking might have something to do with that. Yes, she thought, she was going to have to keep a closer eye on her little sister, especially since she was going to be living so close now. And Kevin won't be able to interfere. That was her fault, letting him dictate so much of her life. Now that she was done with him, she saw how controlling he really was. But you can't always see it when you're in it.

With so much going on in every facet of her life, she needed to put things in their proper perspective. Plus, she needed some fresh air to flush out the smell of cleaning potions and paint fumes. She did her best thinking when she was alone, away from the noise and hectic pace of her life. Pulling on her sneakers and a ball cap, she jogged down the sidewalk and headed toward the high school football field, a short jog from her mom's house.

The earlier sickness that had overcome Jillian was completely gone, but there were a thousand thoughts racing through her head. It probably was stress and exhaustion, as her mom had suggested. Surprisingly, she hadn't thought that much about Kevin after she had gotten over the initial shock of their breakup. At the time, she'd been devastated and cried more than her fair share of tears. His actions and deceit really hurt her and she felt the sting of his betrayal. But she didn't miss him. She missed her job, but her new business venture seemed like it would deliver the same satisfaction and even more as the boss of her career. She and Kevin had grown apart long before they officially ended their relationship, but it was the way it ended that really hurt her. They hadn't talked marriage, but she knew she didn't want to marry Kevin, so the proposal was puzzling. She had even started questioning why they were together in the first place. But building her career had kept Jillian so busy for so long, she hadn't given herself time to focus on her personal life. With their travel schedules being so opposite, they didn't see each other like most couples that live together do. They usually spent part of each weekend together and most times, that was all. They didn't plan and cook dinner together after work, argue about who would clean up and then snuggle together on the couch with a glass of wine before bed. Those were the times she missed. But it was too late to worry about Kevin. She wasn't returning his texts. It surprised her how completely removed she felt from him after being so into him for so long. Guess that meant the breakup was for the best and was final. Her new business venture wouldn't be happening if she were still with Kevin and working at Williams Consulting. She also wouldn't know about Jessica and her struggles, or about the pain that her family went through when she was away. It surprised her how she thought of Jessica as her best friend, but still she knew so little about some very big things.

Now Jillian was stepping out into new, unchartered territory with different challenges to conquer. She felt ready for her meeting with Rick Colbert and was fairly certain he'd like what she was going to propose for his company. She'd already outlined a partial strategy for him, so this meeting was going to be mostly a formality, as they're on the same page. This would give her the chance to talk to him as the business owner, to review schedules, milestones, billing and all of the other details she hadn't been involved in before. They could set goals and projections for the future. It was shaping up to be a challenge, but one that she was ready to embrace, especially since her new office was located in her new house.

Her house. She was a homeowner. It was still hard to believe she would sign the final papers this week. Jillian could hardly contain her excitement at the thought of owning her own house. It was going to be fun decorating the space so it reflected her personal style. She had a lot of ideas and couldn't wait to see them materialize and become real.

Thinking of the house instantly brought Matt into her mind, as she began her second lap around the track at the football field. The irony of thinking about him at this place wasn't lost on her. They shared so many memories here; hanging out with friends, cheering for the football and soccer teams, sitting on the bleachers for hours talking about their dreams and aspirations. She really had been glad to run into him again, and had to admit it saddened her that they hit such a big bump in the road of rekindling their romance from so many years ago. No matter how much she didn't want to admit it, there was still a lot of chemistry between them. It was impossible to deny she was very attracted to him; he'd always had that effect on her heart and her body.

Matt knew her as well as anybody else did and was able to read her like a book. When she was sad or upset about something, he knew and would try to help her work though her problems. He'd been there to share in her victories and her moments of sadness and defeat. She hadn't realized how much she had missed him over the past few years. She remembered hearing an old saying, something like "if you let something go, it will return to you if it was meant to be." Seeing him again, going out with him, made that saying true; except for the fact he was dating someone else.

She tapped the answer button on her headphones as she said hello.

"Jillian, hon, just checking in," Ann said.

Slowing her jog to a walk, she spent time catching up with

her friend.

Talking to Ann always seemed to center her, she thought, starting another lap around the track and noticing the other jogger who was heading right for her. So focused on her call, she hadn't noticed that anyone else was there. The other person slowed down and she had to smile in spite of herself as she recognized the tall, well-built man dressed in old blue gym shorts and a Budweiser Frogs t-shirt. There goes fate again, she couldn't help but smile. Knowing she should be angry and ward off all contact with the opposite sex, it was too exhausting to hold onto those feelings.

"Hi," she gasped, her breath winded. Her muscles burned as she slowly bounced from one foot to the other, willing her heart rate to slow down. Though she knew it wouldn't with him around. And he knew it.

"I'm sorry. Much as I hate to admit it, I was upset by the phone call the other night. Then, seeing you and her together…" she let her voice trail off, not really wanting him to know how much seeing him and Kimberly together had upset her. She wanted Matt back in her life. It was as simple as that, her walls of defense slowly crumbling as his intense stare made her blush. But, she wouldn't let him in if he was involved with someone else. She was too old for that.

"You had a right to be upset, Jilly," Matt said softly. "I should have told you about Kimberly, but she's not a concern anymore."

"What do you mean? You were just at dinner with her the other night," she asked, puzzled by what he was saying. Walking toward the bleachers new the 50-yard line, she sat down, stretching her calves in the process. Taking her lead,

Matt settled on the seat next to her, resting his forearms on his legs and hanging his head so his face was hidden.

"Did you break up?" she asked gently, holding her breath.

"Yep," he sighed, lifting his head to look at her. "It had been a long time coming, then seeing you again and getting pizza, talking about your house…" his voice trailed off. She'd forgotten how incredibly sexy his eyes were, but she instantly recalled as he fixed her with an intense stare.

"Oh Matt, I'm sorry," she said quietly, relating to the emotional turmoil he must be feeling. Her excitement at the prospect embarrassed her as he was clearly as conflicted as she was.

She hated herself for being so selfish, but she liked having Matt back in her life. Shocked that the thought was so firm in her mind, she realized it was true. Looking at him, sitting there, staring at her, she felt nothing but love for the man that her high school sweetheart had become. They'd grown up a lot over the past several years and fate had put them in each other's paths.

Was it just a coincidence?

"Well, what about you? Is this Kevin character out of your life for good?"

"Actually, he tracked me down," she said, smiling at the look of anger that swept his gorgeous features. Hesitating just a second to enjoy his obvious jealousy, she said, "And I told him that it was over, that it had been over and I was moving on with my life." She smiled up at Matt, loving the feelings of desire that swept from her toes straight up to the top of her head whenever he was nearby.

Matt smiled at her, standing up. "Do you want to get out of here?" he asked with a smile, pulling her up beside him. Wrapping his arms around her waist, he said, "You know, I have some great ideas for your house. That is, if you haven't found another contractor.

The ball was in her court, so to speak. It was up to her to either say yes and move forward with the man she loved, or she could walk away and get on with her life without him.

"Do I get a discount because I know the boss?" She asked with a grin as he smiled down at her.

CHAPTER 34

Watching the trees turn shades of red and orange as summer edged into fall, Jillian looked around her yard and admired the space; her sanctuary, her escape when she needed a fresh breath or change of scenery. The new fire pit had already been christened by a marshmallow cookout with Jessie's family, Matt, his sister, Susan, and Kate. She envisioned many more gatherings in her backyard. If she closed her eyes, she could see the snow falling and snowmen dotting the landscape here and there as the seasons continued to turn.

Her backyard wasn't the only thing to go through a metamorphosis of sorts. Jillian herself had changed and, in her estimation, all for the better. The study in her house had evolved into the home office for Simmons Consulting, her very own firm where she had signed not only Rick Colbert's business, but had contracts with two of his colleagues and a developing printing business here in town. Once word had gotten out through local advertising, LinkedIn promotions and dusting off her networking contacts, Jillian was at capacity and had thought about adding a part-time assistant/secretary to help keep up with the paperwork and scheduling. She was busier than she ever thought possible, but she ended her days feeling energized and proud of herself in a way she hadn't felt in a long time.

Jessie was lobbying to fill the role of secretary, but Jillian wanted to keep their relationship separate from her business. Plus, her new role as PTA president at the elementary school was going to keep her pretty busy.

She actually had her eye on one of Jack's tellers at the bank and was considering asking Jack if he thought Betsy Smith, her fellow high school graduate, would be willing to take on the position. The two women had forged a late-blooming friendship as Jillian made Jack's bank her bank. Plus, she and Jessica were PTA parents together, so Betsy was becoming a regular with the Simmons sisters. How funny it was, she thought, that time and distance could change things.

Sitting down on her porch swing on the back deck, she settled into a cadence that had nearly put her to sleep when she heard the backdoor open and softly close. With a smile, she opened her eyes and put a hand over them to shade the bright sun.

"Thought you might want a fresh cup of coffee," Matt said, as he handed her a cup and settled into the seat next to her, continuing the gentle sway of the swing, resting his hand on hers, bringing it to his lips for a light kiss.

Acknowledgements

I'm extremely grateful to my husband, daughters, mother, family and friends for taking me seriously and encouraging me when I shyly shared that I want to publish a novel I started writing several years ago. I couldn't have done this without your love and support.

To my husband, Eli, thank you for your support, encouragement and love. To my daughter, Megan, thank you for pushing me to make my dream a reality and working with me every step of the way. To my daughter, Sarah, your love and support mean the world to me. I don't know where I'd be without you helping keep me grounded. To my mom, thank you for encouraging my reading addiction when I was growing up. To my cousin, Jenny, thank you for always listening and being my sounding board. To my friends and family, thank you for sharing my posts and commenting on my posts with your encouragement. Putting myself out there has been scary and thrilling. Without all of you, I wouldn't have pursued publishing a novel.

Made in the USA
Middletown, DE
29 October 2023